PUBLIC PROFILES

Cristiano Ronaldo

The New York Times

PUBLIC PROFILES

Cristiano Ronaldo

EDUCATIONAL PUBLISHING
BOOKS

THE NEW YORK TIMES EDITORIAL STAFF

Published in 2019 by New York Times Educational Publishing
in association with The Rosen Publishing Group, Inc.
29 East 21st Street, New York, NY 10010

First Edition

The New York Times
Alex Ward: Editorial Director, Book Development
Brenda Hutchings: Senior Photo Editor/Art Buyer
Phyllis Collazo: Photo Rights/Permissions Editor
Heidi Giovine: Administrative Manager

Rosen Publishing
Jacob R. Steinberg: Director of Content Development
Greg Tucker: Creative Director
Brian Garvey: Art Director
Erica Grove: Editor

Cataloging-in-Publication Data
Names: New York Times Company.
Title: Cristiano Ronaldo / edited by the New York Times editorial staff.
Description: New York : New York Times Educational Publishing, 2019. | Series: Public profiles | Includes bibliographic references and index.
Identifiers: ISBN 9781642820164 (pbk.) | ISBN 9781642820157 (library bound) | ISBN 9781642820140 (ebook)
Subjects: LCSH: Ronaldo, Cristiano, 1985- —Juvenile literature. | Soccer players—Portugal—Biography—Juvenile literature.
Classification: LCC GV942.7.R626 C757 2019 | DDC 796.334092 B—dc23

Manufactured in the United States of America

On the cover: Real Madrid's Cristiano Ronaldo during a Champions League match between Real Madrid and Juventus in Madrid, Wednesday, April 11, 2018; Paul White/Associated Press.

Contents

CHAPTER 4

Ronaldo Versus Messi

CHAPTER 5

Controversies and Challenges

CHAPTER 6

Athlete or Celebrity?

Introduction

SINCE THE BEGINNING of his professional career in 2002, Cristiano Ronaldo has distinguished himself as a soccer player and an athlete. In addition to winning five of France Football's Ballon d'Or awards, he is the recipient of 25 trophies for championship and league titles. ESPN named Ronaldo the most famous athlete in the world in 2016 and 2017, and Forbes noted him as the highest paid.

Born February 5, 1985, on the Portuguese island of Madeira as Cristiano Ronaldo dos Santos Aveiro, he came from a humble background. His mother, Dolores, was a cook, and his father, José Dinis, worked as a gardener and equipment manager for the amateur soccer team Andorinha. Although the family lived in poverty, Ronaldo's parents encouraged their son's dream to play soccer. At the age of fourteen, Ronaldo had an altercation with a teacher that resulted in him being expelled from school. At this point, his mother encouraged him to devote himself to soccer, and his father introduced him to the team Andorinha, where Ronaldo's soccer career began.

After playing amateur soccer for four years, Ronaldo tried out for Sporting CP's football academy, to which he was signed for £1500. By the time he was sixteen, Ronaldo was part of the club's youth team and quickly moved up to the Primeira Liga, the top division of the Portuguese national football league. His performance caught the eye of Manchester United, and ultimately the team's manager, Alex Ferguson, offered Ronaldo a position on the team, which he joined when he was eighteen.

Ronaldo distinguished himself playing for Manchester United, winning recognition from the Professional Footballers' Association and Football Writers' Association in the process. In 2008, he was also

IMAGESTOCKDESIGN/SHUTTERSTOCK.COM

Cristiano Ronaldo playing for Real Madrid.

awarded the Premier League Golden Boot and the European Golden Shoe. However, his penchant for theatrical moans and gestures made him seem arrogant and melodramatic. He was accused of faking falls to make it appear as though he were tackled.

Ronaldo's transfer to Real Madrid in 2009 also served as a source of controversy. He openly expressed his desire to join the team while playing for United and was accused of disloyalty. Despite the contentious nature of the transfer, Ronaldo thrived with Real Madrid, gaining more recognition and league titles. By March 18, 2018, Ronaldo had scored 443 goals for Real Madrid, bringing his club career total to 566.

Ronaldo has been accused of being a diva off the field. Some people believe his focus is less on the game and more on his wealth and celebrity, citing his forays into fashion and frequent tabloid appearances as evidence. Others challenge this notion of Ronaldo, pointing out his many philanthropic efforts to improve the lives of the impoverished throughout the world. Regardless of one's opinion about his personality and motives, almost everyone can agree that Ronaldo is one of the most talented players in the history of soccer, with an incredible record to back up this claim.

To be considered the sport's most talented, he must compete with Argentine forward Lionel Messi, who plays for Barcelona and is often compared to Ronaldo. The two often vie for Ballon d'Or awards, FIFA titles, and other top honors, with both tied for a record number of Ballon d'Ors. Because the two players have very different playing styles and personalities yet are almost perfectly matched in titles, they are frequently considered rivals.

This book examines coverage of the various sides of Ronaldo: celebrity, rival, philanthropist, provocateur, and athlete. It explores his major accomplishments, controversies, and events, but also how his public image has been shaped over time, allowing the reader to assess which details ought to shape his enduring legacy.

CHAPTER 1

Early Career: Sporting CP and Manchester United

Nobody knew how famous Cristiano Ronaldo would one day become, but the director of youth recruitment at the Sporting Lisbon academy saw his potential. Ronaldo's skills developed as he moved onto Sporting CP's professional team, along with a reputation for being temperamental. Ronaldo's prowess and competitive nature became increasingly clear when he joined Manchester United. His maneuvering and scoring abilities made him a rising talent, and many viewed him as the star of the team, causing resentment among teammates. Ronaldo transfered to Real Madrid.

Ronaldo's Toughest Move

BY SAM BORDEN | MAY 22, 2014

FUNCHAL, PORTUGAL — The roads of Madeira twist together like licorice ropes, their spindly curves beginning at the seashore and rising up the steps of this steep island in a maze reminiscent of Rio de Janeiro's favelas. The slow climb here comes with a similar feeling to the Brazilian shanties, too: one of utter insulation, a complete removal from the tourist areas that lie below.

That sentiment is fierce within the residents. Last week in Santo Antonio, a parish on the middle of the mountain, two men stood at a table in front of a modest outdoor bar. The men were talking about

Madeira's most famous native, the soccer star Cristiano Ronaldo. But they were not reliving one of Ronaldo's magical goals for Real Madrid nor reveling in one of his epic performances for the national team of Portugal. Rather, they were reminiscing about the time when Ronaldo very nearly ruined his professional career before it ever began.

This happened long before Ronaldo, 29, was a star at Real Madrid, the Spanish giant that will face a city neighbor, Atlético Madrid, in the Champions League final on Saturday. It was before Ronaldo's six years at Manchester United and before he became a global icon and before he was named the captain of Portugal, a role he will continue this summer at the World Cup. The moment the men remembered came when Ronaldo was just a teenager, his godfather, Fernao Sousa, said at the bar. It was when Ronaldo still clung ferociously to that insulation provided by this tiny archipelago known as Pérola do Atlântico, the Pearl of the Atlantic. It was when he did not want to leave.

IMAGESTOCKDESIGN / SHUTTERSTOCK.COM

Cristiano Ronaldo, CR7, Real Madrid player, in action during a Spanish League match between Eibar and Real Madrid in 2018.

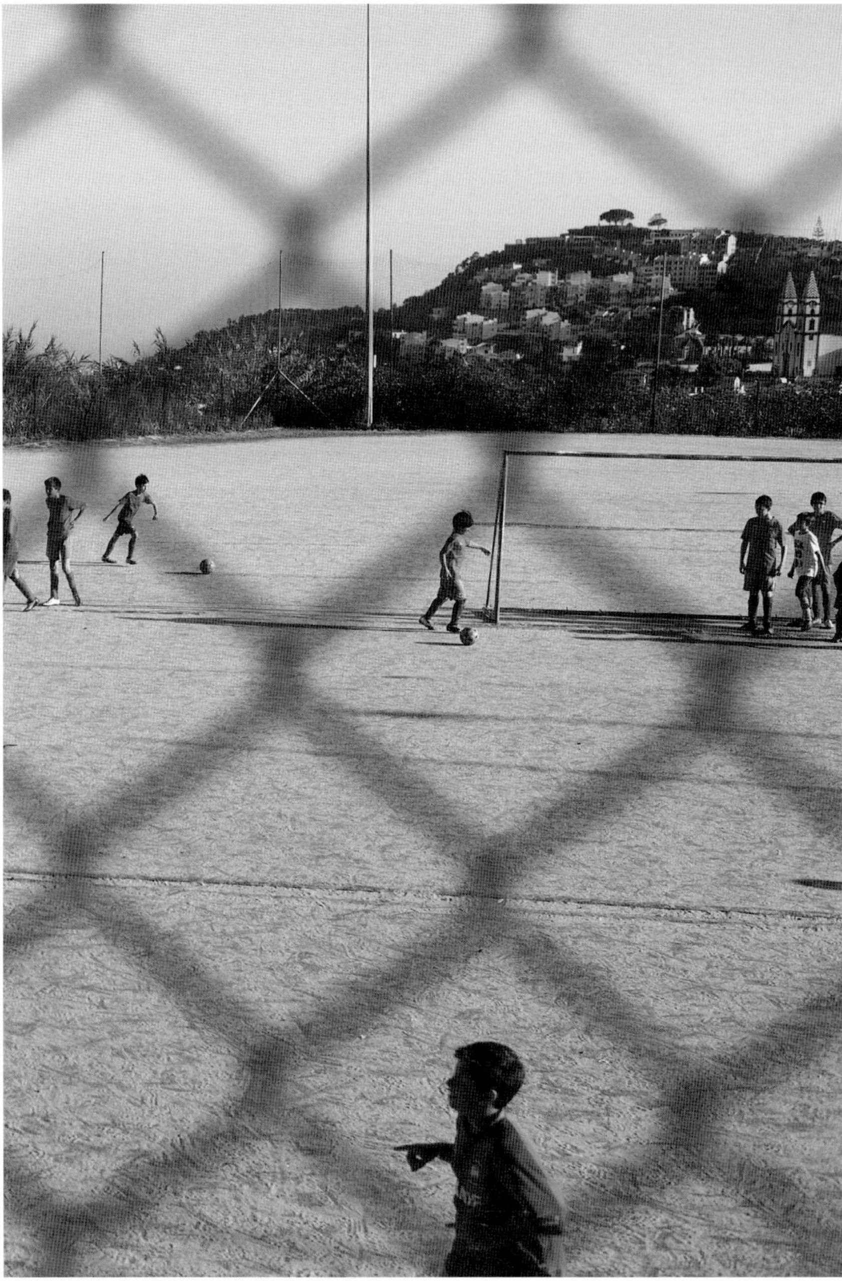

SAMUEL ARANDA FOR THE NEW YORK TIMES

Children training near the neighborhood in Funchal, Portugal, where Cristiano Ronaldo got his start.

"I helped him get to Lisbon," said Sousa, and though he was not referring to Saturday's final at the Estadio da Luz, he might well have been because this week's trip to the Portuguese capital would not have happened without one much earlier. Sousa, of course, was talking about the series of transfers that brought a young Ronaldo from his first club, Andorinha, to a bigger Madeiran club, Nacional, and then finally off the island when he joined the academy of Sporting Lisbon in 1997. Ronaldo was 12. "He was ready," Sousa said.

Sousa, a former player for Andorinha and Nacional himself, had connections that eased Ronaldo's move. He remembered Ronaldo's mother and father being accepting of the opportunity; Ronaldo seemed excited, too. "Your son is your future," Sousa told them.

But a few months into Ronaldo's first season in Lisbon, Sousa heard that his godson was back on the island. Ronaldo was not supposed to be home; the agreement with Sporting allowed for only a few trips back each year, and those were just short visits. Sousa quickly drove the narrow, bumpy roads of Santo Antonio to reach Ronaldo's family house, a tin-roofed, squat three-bedroom for the family of six.

He was told Ronaldo was not happy but did not understand why. Ronaldo loved soccer more than anything. Around Santo Antonio, everyone knew that Ronaldo was always playing, always carrying a ball. "He would skip school just to play," said Ludgero Castro, a long-time neighbor. "His schoolbooks were the soccer ball."

In Lisbon, though, Ronaldo had not found the sanctuary Sousa expected. Ronaldo missed his father, José Dinis, who was a gardener (and the equipment manager for Andorinha's senior team). He missed his mother, Dolores, and his brother and his two sisters. He missed chasing frogs in the dried gullies with his cousin. He missed the familiarity of living in a neighborhood where most of the roofs are an Iberian orange and the streets are one-and-half-cars wide and no one needs to know the names of the roads because every family lives in the same house it has always lived in.

SAMUEL ARANDA FOR THE NEW YORK TIMES

People visiting the Ronaldo museum, which features various memorabilia of the Portuguese star.

He missed, as much as anything, hearing people talk the way he did; in Lisbon, the other boys in the academy taunted him mercilessly, making fun of his Madeiran accent.

He did not want to return to the continent. Sousa and José Dinis, who died in 2005, were not sure what to do.

"We convinced his mother to talk to him," Sousa said, shaking his head. "He always listened to his mother. Then we put him in the car and drove him right to the airport. It was difficult, but he went back."

Sousa smiled. "It is good that he did, no?" he said.

Sousa laughed then, acknowledging his understatement. The bar he was standing at was next to a soccer field with a large photograph of a young Ronaldo, wearing the colors of Andorinha, plastered above the entrance. This field did not exist when Ronaldo was a boy — his first field was a little ways down the hill and "did not even have grass, only dirt," according to Rui Santos, the president of Andorinha when Ronaldo played there. On this island, though, Ronaldo's presence is inescapable.

At the modest airport, advertisements featuring Ronaldo greet passengers as they walk into the terminal. Ask a taxi driver for a "Ronaldo tour" and they will take you to the places of his youth. In Bairro Quinta Falcao, the area where Ronaldo grew up, the cafe his family would go to has pictures of him and one of his jerseys on the wall. "He still comes in when he is visiting," the bartender said. "He likes a full plate of Portuguese fish."

Stop a person on the street in this neighborhood, and they will point to the space just behind Casa Azul, the blue building that serves as a community center. That empty lot is where Ronaldo's childhood house used to stand. The house was torn down several years ago, though residents offer differing accounts why: Some say it was because vandals and vagrants made the house a target after Ronaldo moved his family into a nicer area; others say the Madeiran government, as well as Ronaldo, was concerned that the house projected a poor image of Ronaldo's childhood.

SAMUEL ARANDA FOR THE NEW YORK TIMES

A photo of Ronaldo as a boy hangs at a bar of the Andorinha club, Ronaldo's first team.

Ronaldo's eldest sister, Elma, who operates a Ronaldo-branded clothing store in the more commercial part of Funchal, did not specify why the family's house was demolished. "It was small," she said. "But it was our home. And now things are different."

That was an understatement, too. Ronaldo lives in Madrid now with his girlfriend, a Russian model, and his 3-year-old son. His mother lives near him as well. His other sister, Katia, is a singer. His annual income, according to a recent estimate by Forbes, is $44 million.

Not surprisingly, Ronaldo visits Funchal only "a few times a year," Elma said, and, "whenever he comes he has to be in hiding." There are always visitors, always people who want something. "It is hard for him," she added.

Recently, Ronaldo was here to celebrate the opening of his museum, a sharp gallery near the tourist areas that is dedicated to all things Ronaldo. All kinds of trophies — including random awards, such as one shaped like a ship that was bestowed upon Ronaldo for being the 2003–4 player of the year as voted on by the Scandinavian branch of the Manchester United Supporters Club — are on display, as are jerseys, photographs from Ronaldo's childhood and a collection of match balls from each game during his career in which Ronaldo scored a hat trick.

Ronaldo's cousin, Nuno Viveiros, who lived with Ronaldo while he was playing for Manchester United, runs the museum. Two years older than Ronaldo, Viveiros was the captain of the youth team on which Ronaldo won his first tournament trophy (it is on display at the museum, too). Asked whether he found it at all presumptuous that Ronaldo would want to open a museum while still in the prime of his-career, Viveiros waved his hand.

"He had so many trophies already, it was good for him to display them," Viveiros said. "Plus, he will win more and put them here, too."

That is a common sentiment among Madeirans, who have an unshakable belief in the magic of their favorite player. They remember the days before he was a brash wizard on the field, the days when he

SAMUEL ARANDA FOR THE NEW YORK TIMES

A wax figure of Ronaldo is among the items at his museum. Ronaldo and Real Madrid will play in the Champions League final in Lisbon.

cried after losing games with Andorinha. They remember when his touch with the ball always seemed just a little bit smoother than the other boys.

They remember, too, the time when he did not want to leave.

‘Made in Sporting’: Lisbon Club’s Youth Academy Sets It Apart

BY RORY SMITH | NOV. 21, 2016

LISBON — The way they tell the story at Sporting Lisbon, they did not even have to watch Cristiano Ronaldo play to know he was special. Seeing him with a ball at his feet, the quiet, skinny 12-year-old’s every effortless touch proof of his masterly control, was enough.

Pretty much everyone at Sporting knows the tale, which is now part of the club’s folklore; pretty much everyone tells it in the same way, with a cadence and cast of characters seemingly straight out of the Nativity. It even features three wise men.

Early in 1997, the president of Sporting’s fan club on the island of Madeira got in touch with Aurélio Pereira, the Lisbon club’s long-serving director of youth recruitment. There was, he said, a prodigiously gifted child in the academy ranks at Nacional, one of three professional clubs in the island’s capital, Funchal.

Pereira, wily and mustachioed, duly sent a scout to assess the claims. The prodigy in question was scheduled to play in a tournament for Nacional. When Sporting’s emissary arrived, though, he discovered his target was not scheduled to participate. He found him, instead, on the sideline, alone with a ball, thoroughly absorbed as he went through his repertory of flicks and feints. The emissary watched for a while.

He did not know then that Ronaldo would go on to become one of the finest players in history, a three-time winner of the World Player of the Year Award, a three-time winner of the Champions League, a champion of Europe with Portugal and, for a while, the world’s most expensive player. But he knew enough. The scout called Pereira and told him to invite Ronaldo to Lisbon, immediately, for a trial.

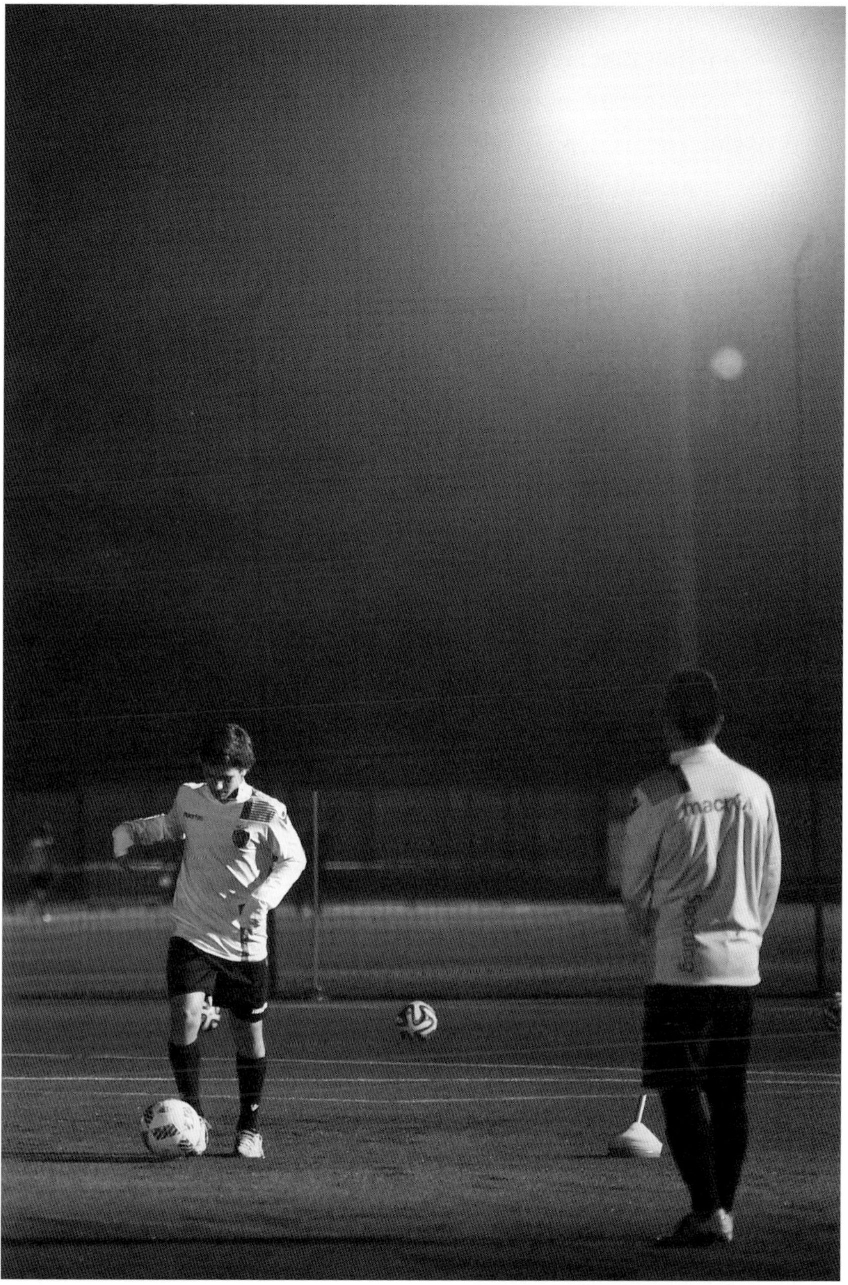

PATRICIA DE MELO MOREIRA FOR THE NEW YORK TIMES

Young soccer players trained at Sporting Lisbon's productive youth academy in Alcochete, Portugal.

Nearly 20 years after Ronaldo's arrival — and 13 since his departure — Sporting Lisbon remains tremendously proud of all that Ronaldo has become. His image has been emblazoned on a mural outside the dressing rooms deep inside Sporting's Estádio José Alvalade, and the club's fans will offer a lavish welcome when he takes to the field for Real Madrid, against Sporting, in the Champions League on Tuesday. He will be left with little doubt as to just how much he means to them.

An hour away, in Pereira's office at Sporting's youth academy at Alcochete, the reverence is similar. The walls are littered with pictures of Ronaldo, and two signed shirts from his days at Manchester United hang behind the director's desk. Pereira still reels through his memories with glee.

He remembers giving a team talk, only to look to his side and find Ronaldo, bored and impatient, juggling a bottle of water with his feet. He recalls the nights when Ronaldo and his friend José Semedo would vault a wall and break into the gym to do some impromptu — and strictly forbidden — weight training.

Pereira's favorite memory is the one involving a traffic light on Praça do Marquês de Pombal. "It was near where the young players used to live," Pereira said in an interview Friday. "Ronaldo would go and wait by the stop sign. There is a ramp immediately after it. Ronaldo would tie weights to his legs, and wait for the light to turn green. Then he would race the cars up the ramp."

But while Ronaldo might have a rare prominence here, he is not the only player whose photo graces that office wall. Dozens of other players are featured, too: curling, yellowing shots of Paulo Futre and Luís Figo, more recent images of Nani and of Simão Sabrosa, as well as fresh printouts of Portugal's victorious Euro 2016 team, the majority of players in full color, a handful rendered in gray.

Everyone at Sporting knows why: Of the 14 players Portugal used in that final against France, 10 were "made in Sporting."

PATRICIA DE MELO MOREIRA FOR THE NEW YORK TIMES

From left, Luís Martins, Alcochete's technical coordinator; Aurélio Pereira, Sporting's longtime director of recruitment; and Virgílio Lopes, the director of the youth academy, regularly welcome visitors interested in the secret to producing top-flight soccer players.

PATRICIA DE MELO MOREIRA FOR THE NEW YORK TIMES

Pereira's office also features other memorabilia like, from left, Ronaldo's Manchester United jersey, Nani's Manchester United jersey and Ronaldo's Real Madrid jersey.

Ronaldo is Pereira's greatest find, but he is far from the only one. Alcochete, as Sporting's academy is known, is regarded by the International Center for Sports Studies as a more productive academy than those at Barcelona, Real Madrid and Manchester United.

By one metric, only three clubs (Ajax, Partizan Belgrade and Dinamo Zagreb) have more graduates playing top-flight soccer in Europe than Sporting. The story of how Ronaldo came to Lisbon might be told like a fairy tale, but it is better read as a case study as to what, exactly, sets Sporting apart.

"We do not have any secrets," said Virgílio Lopes, the director of the academy.

His actions back up his words: Clubs from across the world regularly visit Sporting to find out what lies behind its success rate. They are welcomed by Lopes, Pereira and Luís Martins, Alcochete's technical coordinator.

PATRICIA DE MELO MOREIRA FOR THE NEW YORK TIMES

Players gathered to start a training session at Sporting's youth academy in Alcochete.

"We tell them everything we can," Lopes said. "Well, we tell them almost everything we can."

They tell them, for example, the atmosphere they seek to create: free-range players, not battery-caged ones, in Pereira's chicken farming analogy. "They are young people who play football; they are not just small footballers," Lopes said. "We do not want them to be professional at 14. We want them to still be professional at 20."

They tell them that they stick to what they do, what they have always done, rather than changing.

And they open up their training models, too, explaining how everything is tailored to the individual. "We find the strong and weak points of each player," Martins said. "Every player needs different things, so we change their training schedules to reflect that."

That applies in the gym, where each player has a customized conditioning plan, and on the field. "If a player is having difficulty making good passes, we will change the training they do," Martins said.

Sporting's staff also incorporates less traditional elements. "We play football-squash and foot-volley using the walls," Martins said. "It helps with open decision making."

There is no Barcelona-style template for what system or shape to play. "We don't find that important," Martins said. "Things get more complex as they get older. They need to be able to play in different scenarios because that is what professionals have to do."

There is only one thing they do not tell their visitors, the one thing that everyone at the club identifies as its key advantage, its greatest weapon.

"Recruitment is the first thing," Martins said. And nobody is better at recruiting than Sporting, as the parable of Cristiano Ronaldo demonstrates, because nobody else can call on Pereira.

A 50-year veteran at Sporting — as player, coach and now scout — Pereira was the man responsible for setting up the club's youth recruitment department in 1987. He built a database of the most talented young players in Portugal by writing to every single Sporting

PATRICIA DE MELO MOREIRA FOR THE NEW YORK TIMES

In Pereira's office at Sporting's youth academy in Alcochete hangs a bulletin board containing pictures of players he has worked with through the years.

socio, or member, in the country, all 96,000 of them, and asking them to recommend any prospects in their local area.

Once he had collated the replies, Pereira set about acquiring more information.

"I spoke to coaches, referees, firemen, policemen about the most promising," he said. "We brought the best of them to Lisbon to train. That was how we became the first club in the country to organize youth scouting at the national level."

It is also, of course, how he built a network so reliable that having heard about a promising 12-year-old player on an island closer to the African coast than to Lisbon, the president of a fan club might write to headquarters advising it to take a look. It is how he distilled the approach so finely that a scout did not need to see the youngster play to know he was worth pursuing.

And it is how he built a system that unearthed not only Ronaldo, but also all those who came before, and all those who have continued to come after.

The Rain and the Minutes Pelt Down

BY GEORGE VECSEY | MAY 22, 2008

FIRST THE CALVES CRAMP UP, then the mind. How else to explain the pitty-pat slap that Didier Drogba administered in the final slogging minutes of the Champions League final on Wednesday?

Does the name Zinédine Zidane strike a familiar chord?

With one master imitating another, another dreaded shootout mimicking the head-butt World Cup final of 2006, Manchester United beat Chelsea after a 1-1 draw in the rain of Moscow.

The slap by Drogba happened during one of those milling-about scrums that take place when players have lost their marbles late in a match. This obvious weariness of leg and gray matter explains why championship games must end somehow after 120 minutes rather than have these exhausted athletes milling around any longer.

For most of the match, there was a simple plot. Cristiano Ronaldo, still only 23, was obviously the best player on the soggy turf, which had been imported from Slovakia. Ronaldo had the best moves, skippy little stutter-steps that allowed him to get around defenders time and again. The whole match was predicated on Ronaldo, the handsome Portuguese youth with No. 7 on his back, and double joints in his ankles and knees.

I was watching the match in BXL Cafe, a Belgian place on West 43rd Street, but thinking of the shuttered L'Angolo in Greenwich Village, where we used to watch this final. BXL was jammed with a good percentage of Americans who talked knowledgeably about players and strategy. And many neutral observers, eating moules and frites and drinking Belgian beer, hissed at Ronaldo's diving theatrics while admiring his magnificent talent.

Not only can the kid run and jump, he has also mastered heading the ball, which seems almost unfair. On Wednesday, in the 26th minute, he worked his way to the back post and outleapt a defender to convert a cross from Wes Brown that gave Manchester United a 1-0 lead. The goal was his 42nd of this season.

The place went nuts for reflexive saves by Edwin van der Sar, the Dutch keeper for Man U, and Peter Cech, the Czech keeper for Chelsea. (For this first Champions League final between two English clubs, they flew all the way to Moscow to represent the Russian owner of Chelsea and the American owner of United.)

Chelsea managed to draw even in the 45th minute, when Frank Lampard scavenged a loose ball and flipped it past van der Sar and pointed to the heavens in honor of his mother, who died earlier this spring.

In the second half, Chelsea began to use all the tools put at Coach Avram Grant's disposal by the very wealthy friend-of-Putin owner, Roman Abramovich. Drogba became more noticeable up front. Michael Essien began to make sorties from the deep right, where he had been shadowing Ronaldo. In the 78th minute, Drogba hit the right post.

The minutes added up, cramping everybody's brilliance. In overtime, Lampard hit a crossbar at 94 minutes and John Terry, the stalwart Chelsea captain, stuck his head in the way of Ryan Giggs's shot in the 101st minute.

By then, the players were fried. Those who were not lying on the ground, stretching their calves, were lurching into one another, looking for trouble, out too late, too far from home, like punch-drunk sailors in a foreign port.

Drogba chose to make his effete little slap in the open field, just as the smooth Zidane of France had delivered a head-butt to Italy's Marco Materazzi late in the World Cup final in 2006 after a slur of some kind. Zidane was expelled then and Drogba was banished now.

Just as Zidane was not available for the shootout in 2006, with no guarantee he would have scored, Drogba was not available in the miserable little coda of the shootout that soccer uses, because there is no more logical or humane solution for a draw.

The mood in the cafe changed when Ronaldo sauntered in for his penalty kick and kissed the ball. Only a few closeted United fans did not hoot and jeer at the gesture. Virtual unity on West 43rd Street. When Cech guessed right and smothered Ronaldo's low shot, the joint laughed derisively.

But the plot kept spinning as Terry, the anti-Ronaldo, tall and stoic, botched the fifth Chelsea attempt, and Nicolas Anelka missed the seventh one, and Sir Alex Ferguson had his second championship, and United had its third, and the long European season was over.

Everybody now gets to take a deep breath. The frolics resume with Euro 2008 from June 7-29 in Austria and Switzerland, the second-greatest soccer tournament in the world, often won by dashing outsiders. Even American soccer has three big friendlies coming up: England at Wembley on May 28, Spain at Santander on June 4, and Argentina at Giants Stadium on June 8. Good grief, even the Red Bulls are showing signs of resolve.

Soccer never really sleeps on this planet. For a few days, soccer buffs can relive the pageant of Cristiano Ronaldo dominating a muddy pitch, defying the gods with an ostentatious smooch of the ball, and finally rolling on the grass in relief.

Ronaldo Struts Across Big Stage

BY ROB HUGHES | MAY 5, 2009

LONDON — Sport at its finest has elements of the Colosseum, and it is apt that most theatrical of players, Cristiano Ronaldo, has booked Manchester United's place in Rome for the Champions League final later this month.

Ronaldo is a leading player on any stage. He created one goal, then scored two of greatly differing nature in Manchester United's emphatic 3-1 victory at Arsenal on Tuesday. His was the commanding performance that took United to Europe's grand finale for the second year running.

But as much as he loves the spotlight, the finest aspect of Ronaldo is that he knows how to play the team game, and when to step up to his own match-winning moments of virtuosity.

He is close, now, to those outstanding performers of yesteryear — Alfredo di Stéfano, Johan Cruyff, Pelé, Diego Maradona and, in a Manchester United context, George Best. Each of them had star quality, each could make the difference, and each knew that skill without effort was counterproductive.

There was a moment Tuesday when Ronaldo made time stand still and hushed an audience of 60,000 Arsenal supporters.

It arrived in the 11th minute. Manchester was a goal up, thanks to a slick pass from Ronaldo, a slip by Kieran Gibbs, Arsenal's teenage defender, and a smart finish by Park Ji-sung.

Then came Ronaldo's spellbinding solo act. He artfully won a free kick, and devastatingly scored from it. But the whole sequence was pure performance.

The night was young, an almost full moon shone over Emirates Stadium, and Ronaldo took up his free-kick pose. He stood statuesque, the ball in front of him, legs wide apart, arms splayed stiffly at his side.

He seemed to summon the crowd's silence, to address the ball as if there is something secretive between man and object. His face was the picture of concentration.

Then from maybe 10 paces behind the ball, he ran up and struck it with his right boot.

Maybe Manuel Almunia, Arsenal's goalkeeper, was a fraction slow in moving to his left. Maybe he was astonished by the flight of the ball. Anyway, he was beaten.

And so, after barely 10 minutes' action, was Arsenal.

None of this is accident or surprise. Ronaldo's teammates testify to his habit of staying behind after training, day after day perfecting these free kicks, turning fantasy into art.

"I know the shot is quite difficult to save, because the ball moves about," he said. "I have a goalkeeper with me in training, and when they go in, it's not easy for him."

Handling Ronaldo is not easy, period. He is 24, and Alex Ferguson, his manager at Manchester United, has spent six years finding ways to get the best out of him.

Last summer, after Ronaldo also scored a different type of goal, a header in the Champions League final against Chelsea in Moscow, his head and his heart were being wooed by Real Madrid.

Ferguson talked his player out of going to Spain, but there have been periods when Ronaldo appears to brood, to hanker, perhaps, for Madrid.

That club, after all, was his boyhood dream. He grew up in southern Europe, on the Portuguese island of Madeira. He was born with skills and blessed with the physique of a young Adonis. Before his father could know all of that, he christened the boy Cristiano Ronaldo dos Santos Aveiro.

The second name is significant. His father was a fan of Ronald Reagan's acting, so maybe the son was predestined to be something of a thespian.

An actor, a player, a very fine dead-ball specialist.

There is so much more.

SAMUEL ARANDA FOR THE NEW YORK TIMES

The Portuguese island of Madeira, where Ronaldo was born.

To outfox Arsenal, to exploit a lack of pace in the heart of its defense, Ferguson deployed Ronaldo at center forward rather than in his customary role as a winger.

It worked because Ronaldo's inventive mind took it as license to roam where instinct led him. Arsenal's defenders sought him here, there and everywhere.

Because United has so many other fine players, creators and unselfish runners as well, this freedom is amplified. The coup de grâce came with a goal after 61 minutes that was the opposite of Ronaldo's still-life free kick routine.

The ball was moved rapidly and precisely from back to front, the length of the playing surface, in less than a third of a minute.

Nemanja Vidic headed it out of defense. Ronaldo flicked it backward with his heel to set Park sprinting forward. Park made an incisive pass from the center circle to the left. Wayne Rooney then ran with the ball, urgently and swiftly toward goal.

Instead of shooting, Rooney chose to pass. Who did he pick out? Why, Ronaldo. He had not stopped running, and was there to finish off the sweeping counterattack with his instep.

Arsenal's team, gifted but on this occasion outsmarted and outclassed, gained a late consolation with a penalty goal that demonstrated the other side of soccer's human drama.

Cesc Fàbregas stole into the United area but was caught by Darren Fletcher. In a desperate tackle, a lunge from behind, Fàbregas fell.

Fletcher is one of United's workhorses, a selfless runner who never tires of shuttling between defense and attack. His attempt to win the ball was partly successful and his right foot, raised above waist height, did deflect the ball before Fàbregas could shoot.

Fletcher's momentum carried him through Fàbregas and felled the Arsenal man. A penalty, and a red card, said the referee, Roberto Rosetti of Italy.

Fletcher's act was rash. It isn't Rosetti who makes the law that a tackle from behind, preventing a goal, merits an automatic red card. It isn't in the referee's realm to rescind the punishment, even though it becomes a triple punishment. The card and the penalty did not change the result; that was not in doubt. But Fletcher will be banned for United's next European match: the Champions League final.

Before and after that, speculation is bound to grow that Madrid still covets Ronaldo. Ferguson will continue to tell the player that, at 24, his peak is yet to come and nowhere is better for him than at a club that is winning, and defending, all the trophies.

Should Ronaldo go, United is reported to want Franck Ribéry, the French winger at Bayern Munich. Fine individualist that Ribéry sometimes is, a winger is no replacement for a man who can play anywhere in a team that knows how to liberate him.

The longevity of Alex Ferguson's 25 years as Manchester United's manager contrasts sharply with news that Jürgen Klinsmann, Marco van Basten and Felix Magath are all moving on from their posts.

Klinsmann was fired by Bayern Munich last week. Van Basten quit a three-year commitment to his club, Ajax Amsterdam, on Wednesday. Magath is moving from Wolfsburg to Schalke at the season's end.

All three arrived in management or coaching after more glittering playing careers than Ferguson. They are among the thousands who are unlikely to ever experience the continuity that has helped the Scot sustain Manchester's place at the summit of the sport.

Van Basten's departure mirrors that of Klinsmann, even though the Dutchman went willingly. They both are relatively young men whose playing prime we will not readily forget, and both fell victim to expectations that their scoring touch would translate into victories as coaches.

According to the Ajax club statement issued Wednesday, Van Basten "reached the conclusion that he had failed to achieve the goals he set out at the start of the season and would be unable to do any better next season." Ajax is third behind Alkmaar and Twente in the Dutch first division.

Its heyday as a kindergarten club that produced Van Basten, Frank Rijkaard and so many more memorable players is a mere memory. The formula of hiring former players to pass on their knowledge falls down unless the caliber of apprentices is renewed.

Magath's story, however, is different. He is quitting Wolfsburg, currently the leader of the Bundesliga, to take over at seventh-place Schalke. "I regret the timing," Magath said, acknowledging that the announcement was unusual as Wolfsburg has a chance of winning the German championship for the first time.

"There are good reasons," the onetime German and Hamburg creative midfielder said. "The goals I agreed to at the beginning with Wolfsburg's board have been reached. Nobody believed we would achieve that within two years together."

Wolfsburg and Magath both suggest that he overachieved, and that is why a wealthier but underachieving Schalke wants him. With four games left in the season, he could win a championship that nobody predicted and move onward and upward.

Magath was dismissed from his previous post, at Bayern Munich, after twice winning the league and cup double. He walks away from his present team on the cusp of both coaching and managing it to the title.

"We offer our thanks to Mr. Magath for his extraordinary achievement in such a short period of time," said Hans-Dieter Poetsch, chairman of the Wolfsburg board.

Dazzling Ronaldo Leaves Arsenal Gasping for Air

BY ROB HUGHES | MAY 5, 2009

LONDON — Cristiano Ronaldo shot Manchester United to its second successive European Champions League final on Tuesday night. He created an early goal, then scored two as United comfortably beat Arsenal, 3-1, at Emirates Stadium and won the two-leg semifinal on aggregate, 4-1.

United advanced to the final May 27 in Rome, where it will play Chelsea or Barcelona. Those teams play the second leg of their semifinal on Wednesday at Stamford Bridge in London; their first match ended in a scoreless tie.

United's victory Tuesday reflected its mastery, which stemmed from its greater know-how throughout the team. Yet if ever there was a player born to stardom, it is Cristiano Ronaldo dos Santos Aveiro.

His father gave him the second name Ronaldo because he liked Ronald Reagan as an actor. Ronaldo, who was born on the Portuguese island Madeira, has been accused of possessing the thespian. There is also athleticism, great skill and a growing appreciation of team play.

Ronaldo generally plays wing, but United Manager Sir Alex Ferguson sprang a surprise by asking him to play central striker. In Ronaldo's inventive mind, that gave him a license to roam wherever instinct took him.

In the eighth minute, he raced past Johan Djourou down the left side and passed the ball along the ground to Park Ji-Sung in the Arsenal penalty area. Just as Park received the ball, Arsenal defender Kieran Gibbs lost his footing on grass that was slick after being watered to enable the ball to roll. Park received the pass and scored.

Less than four minutes later, Ronaldo artfully won a free kick, and devastatingly scored from it.

United's players testify to the effort that Ronaldo puts into combining power, precision and trajectory on his free kicks.

Before Ronaldo takes free kicks, he assumes a stance that is theatrical, bordering on arrogant. His arms are spread, his face locked in concentration. Upon the referee's whistle, he runs 10 paces and hits the ball in such a way that it gathers speed as it dips toward the goal.

Maybe Arsenal goalkeeper Manuel Almunia moved toward his left a fraction too late. Maybe he was astonished by the flight of the ball. Anyway, he was beaten.

"The shot was quite difficult to save because the ball moved a little bit," Ronaldo said. "I just try to do my best to put the ball in the net and it was a good goal."

So, after barely 10 minutes of play, the euphoric atmosphere inside Emirates Stadium was flattened.

"We do not have the feeling that we played a semifinal in the Champions League because it was over after 10 minutes," Arsenal Manager Arsène Wenger said. "The most disappointing thing is that the game was over before it even started."

The coup de grâce came in the 61st minute. Manchester's third goal was a classic breakaway, a sweeping move the length of the field. Nemanja Vidic headed the ball clear of his penalty area, Ronaldo flicked the ball onward with a backheel, then Park passed it through the central area, and Wayne Rooney accelerated down the left.

When Rooney was ready, who should be sprinting into the Arsenal area? Ronaldo, of course. The finish, with Ronaldo's instep, was his 25th goal of this season in all competitions, his 67th in two seasons.

The only negative for United came in the 75th minute when defender Darren Fletcher was issued a red card for a tackle from behind on Cesc Fàbregas in the penalty area. Robin van Persie converted the penalty kick, and Fletcher will miss the final.

Ronaldo Is Bound for Madrid

BY JACK BELL | JUNE 11, 2009

A WORLD-RECORD TRANSFER fee of more than $131 million has persuaded Manchester United to let Cristiano Ronaldo go to Real Madrid.

Early Thursday, the champion of the English Premier League and runner-up to Barcelona in the European Champions League said on its Web site that it would accede to the wishes of the player, who is Portuguese, and accept the latest and greatest bid from the Spanish powerhouse club.

Ronaldo, 24, a skillful and swift wing who wears the coveted No. 7 jersey worn by United greats like George Best and Eric Cantona, tried to engineer a transfer to Real Madrid during the off season last year, but United angrily rebuffed overtures from Spain. Now, obviously, things have changed, and United has grown weary of the battle for one of the most popular and controversial players in the club's long and storied history. He will receive a percentage of the transfer fee, in addition to any contract his representatives negotiate with Real Madrid.

United's Web site said: "At Cristiano's request — who has again expressed his desire to leave — and after discussion with the player's representatives, United have agreed to give Real Madrid permission to talk to the player. Matters are expected to be concluded by 30 June."

The record transfer of Ronaldo trumps by only days the previous record-high transfer fee of $92 million that Real Madrid paid A.C. Milan of Italy for the Brazilian star Kaká.

Cristiano Ronaldo dos Santos Aveiro, who hails from Madeira, an archipelago in the Atlantic Ocean, joined United in 2003 from Sporting Club Lisbon on a transfer fee of nearly $20 million. The amount paid by Real Madrid represents a tidy profit for United that will enable it to add several more players. Last summer, he lobbied hard for a transfer to Real Madrid, calling it his "dream move."

Ronaldo. who is under contract until 2012, again put his future with

United in doubt after a loss last month to Barcelona in the final of the European Champions League in Rome. After the match, Ronaldo said he could not guarantee that he would remain with the Red Devils. Cue the speculation.

Real Madrid, which like its top domestic rival Barcelona will tour North America this summer, is desperate to reclaim the La Liga title. Seeing Barcelona win both the league and the Champions League titles never sits well in the Spanish capital. Real Madrid won back-to-back titles in 2006-7 and 2007-8 after a three-year drought.

Ronaldo scored 118 goals in 292 games in all competitions for Manchester United, with his best season coming in 2007-8 when he scored 42 goals.

Was this move inevitable? Does the addition of Ronaldo once again make Real Madrid the team to beat in Spain and the world? Who will replace him at Manchester United?

Ronaldo to Join Real Madrid for Record Price

BY ROB HUGHES | JUNE 11, 2009

LONDON — Cristiano Ronaldo, world player of the year in soccer in 2008, is poised to join Ricardo Kaká at Real Madrid, completing a lavish outlay by the Spanish club of more than €159 million for two of the best players in the world.

On Thursday, Manchester United, the English Premier League champion, announced that it had accepted €94 million, or $131.5 million, to sell Ronaldo to Real Madrid — the highest transfer fee in soccer. The move comes three days after Real Madrid tied up its €65 million bid for the Brazilian star Kaká from A.C. Milan.

Real Madrid will now negotiate terms with Ronaldo, a 24-year-old Portuguese midfielder. The Real Madrid president, Florentino Pérez, said he expected to reach agreement in a few days, and Pérez is known as an executive who gets his man.

Ronaldo will command at least the salary of Kaká, €9.1 million a year. Both players will share with Real Madrid income the club gets in shirt and product sales using their images.

Once Ronaldo's contract is written — by June 30, according to Manchester United — it will value one player more highly than the entire amount that Newcastle United, an English club, has been put on the market for.

Real Madrid could make it three in a week by concluding the purchase of David Villa, the Spanish striker who plays for Valencia and is likely to be the top goal scorer available. Madrid and Valencia are haggling over the fee, but it will not be less than €38 million.

The deals leave no doubt that Madrid is on a mission. It is prepared to spend €250 million on player transactions, defying the global financial squeeze. It clearly signals the flamboyant return of Pérez as the club's president.

He was the man behind the showy acquisition of the so-called Galacticos — the superstars Zinédine Zidane, Luís Figo, David Beckham and Robinho. Pérez, a billionaire construction magnate, said there was no price too high for the finest players — and no price he could not recoup by marketing them.

"Real Madrid must dismiss all doubt to be considered the most prestigious sports institution in the world," he declared on the day he was re-elected Madrid's president on June 1.

Ronaldo epitomizes Pérez's concept of a marketable superstar. He is sculpted and good-looking. He is an exciting attacking player, one whose audacity with the ball bewitches the audience.

Though Ronaldo is among the best several players in the world, Madrid's offer clearly proved too tempting for Malcolm Glazer and his sons, the Florida family that owns Manchester United. The BBC reported on its Web site that a spokesman for the family said the decision to sell Ronaldo was taken solely by the manager, Alex Ferguson.

"It was purely a football decision and had nothing to do with the financial structure of the club," the spokesman said.

Ronaldo had wanted to join Madrid last season, angering many Manchester United fans, but was persuaded to stay for one more year. Manchester's announcement of the deal made blunt reference to Ronaldo's desire to move on, saying: "At Cristiano's request — he has again expressed his desire to leave — and after discussion with the player's representatives, United have agreed to give Real Madrid permission to talk to the player. Matters are expected to be concluded by 30 June."

There were news reports in Spain that if Real failed to sign him this month, it would have to pay the Portuguese player and his agent €30 million in compensation.

Manchester United has declined comment beyond its statement, but Ferguson is surely already casting around for replacements.

Ronaldo's ego was growing at United. His detractors cited his tendency to act alone, and to brood when substituted, traits that became potentially divisive. Critics believe he played for himself rather than the club the night United lost its Champions League crown to Barcelona last month.

There lies the crux of the sale. Madrid, in a three-year downturn, wants him to help win Europe's greatest tournament. It is competing with its rival, Barcelona, which has the other top star in the world, Lionel Messi, as well as two top homegrown players, Andrés Iniesta and Xavi Hernández.

So with the money chasing too few match winning performers, Ferguson is expected to pursue the purchase of two or more players who, together, might help the team overcome the loss of Ronaldo. He would like the French winger Franck Ribery, but his club Bayern Munich will raise the asking price with the Ronaldo money in mind. United would find it easier to buy the Ecuadorean winger Antonio Valencia. Fast, tricky, as yet untested at the level of Champions League, Valencia currently plays for the English club Wigan. He would fetch up to €20 million on the market.

Pérez is not spending his own money. He is an elected president, installed by the 75,000 members who pay to belong to Real Madrid in all its sporting interests, from soccer to basketball. The bulk of the money comes from Real's ability to negotiate its own separate television rights, from the membership subscription, from ticket sales, and marketing.

But Pérez, a former politician as well as businessman, has managed to persuade banks to make millions of euros in loans that back his judgment on players.

Ronaldo was born on the Portuguese island of Madeira and always claimed that his mother particularly dreamed of her son playing in the all-white uniform of Real Madrid.

It is a matchup of the most glamorous champion team in the European Cup — now the Champions League — and a winger who craves to be the best.

His physique is strong as well as lithe. His "step overs" — using one foot and then the other over the ball at full speed — are breathtaking.

His ability to strike free kicks from 40 meters, about 125 feet, to induce power and bend on the ball, eclipses even that of Beckham.

During the 2007-2008 season, in which Manchester won the English Premier League and the European Champions League, Ronaldo scored 42 goals.

Beckham was also sold by Manchester United to Real Madrid — in 2003, for £24 million. But Beckham does not have the skills to compare to Ronaldo, no pace, no ability to constantly astound. No winger since George Best, at Manchester United in the 1960s and early '70s, has had such scoring potential. Despite a serious ankle injury at the start of the 2009 season, he has proven his versatility as a center forward who could, among other things, leap high to score in the air.

The followers of Real Madrid will know that their president covets attacking players at all costs. His failure to acknowledge the importance of defenders, however, is legend, and the lack of balance undid the team he built, or bought, during his first term as president, from 2000 to 2006.

So far, Pérez has reverted to type and chased attacking performers. Kaká is the most complete playmaker in world soccer, a man who makes others play by his passes and his vision. Ronaldo is a performer on the flank, down the center, in attacks or in midfield. Villa, if Madrid closes that deal, too, is an out-and-out striker, a finisher.

These players, and whoever else Madrid fields with them, will be handed over to Manuel Pellegrini, who was coaching the provincial Spanish club Villarreal until Real's president signed him a week ago. Pellegrini will be handed the ingredients, and sink or swim with a collection of players more gifted than any he has commanded before.

Ronaldo Leaves His Old Team in Awe

BY ROB HUGHES | FEB. 14, 2013

LONDON — It was a night of joy and dread. Cristiano Ronaldo had soared above his former team, Manchester United, to head a fantastic goal for Real Madrid. It was a prodigious leap, a header that will be remembered by a television audience estimated at 200 million worldwide.

But thousands of kilometers away in Ukraine, the other Champions League match, between Shakhtar Donetsk and Borussia Dortmund, began Wednesday in somber silence.

A small charter plane carrying 44 passengers and crew, among them fans heading to the game, overshot the runway and burst into flames. Five were reported dead and 12 injured.

If there is one club that travels with sadder memories of February, it is Manchester United. Its youngest — and some say best — team, the Busby Babes, was wiped out when its aircraft crashed at Munich airport on a refueling stop from a European match in Belgrade in 1958.

To this day, the clock outside Manchester's Old Trafford stadium is stopped at the moment of the disaster.

Yet the club rebuilt, and it recruited over and over again some of the finest players the world has seen.

One of those, undoubtedly, was Ronaldo. United took him from Portugal when he was 18, enjoyed him for six years, then sold him for a world record fee of £80 million, about $125 million, to Real Madrid in 2009. It was not a parting that United Manager Alex Ferguson enjoyed or could do anything to prevent.

Ronaldo is that rare creature in the sport who can determine his own heart's desire. As a child in Madeira, Portugal, following the Galácticos, he had imagined himself playing in the all-white uniform of Real. It was about fortune, but even more about fame.

The talent is his. Ferguson taught him how to use it, matured him like Madeira wine. There was, Ferguson thought, nothing Cristiano could do that would astonish him.

Nothing until the 30th minute of the Wednesday game at the Santiago Bernabéu. Let the United manager tell it as he saw it: "What a header!" he said. "You can't stop that.

"The leap, the spring, the way he held himself in the air. Unbelievable. When Cristiano gets the ball, you're praying more than anything else."

Ferguson admitted that at halftime he had asked Patrice Evra, his captain and the nearest opponent to Ronaldo in that instant, why he had not challenged in the air. "Then I saw the replay," the manager added. "And I thought, Christ, what was I talking about?"

The leap, the hang, was reminiscent of the athletic agility of basketball's Michael "Air" Jordan.

The power in the spring apparently comes from the quads. The strength to hold in the air, and at the propitious moment to coil the torso and apply his head like a hammer to the ball, is all Ronaldo's.

No goalkeeper could reach it. David De Gea, a Spaniard representing United back in his home city, was in the form of his life in Manchester's jersey. De Gea had earlier flung himself to the full extent of his 1.90 meter, or 6-foot-3, frame and reach to diverted a low shot from Ángel Di María.

But this header, this athletic perfection, would not be denied by anyone.

Ronaldo's celebration was muted. He put his fingers to his lips and directed kisses to the crowd. To Madridistas, or apologetically to Mancunians? We could not tell.

But after the contest, which ended all square at 1-1, Ronaldo was drawn to his old pals in the United dressing room. He had done his job, scoring a vital, and a great, goal against people he had shared six years of his life with. But now, with the two-leg tie poised at what is effectively halftime, human considerations outweighed professional rivalry.

The tournament arguably means more to Madrid than it does to Manchester. Real has neglected the Spanish league and virtually given up on defending its domestic title against the superior Barcelona.

Real's coach, José Mourinho, is a Champions League specialist, and only the Champions League remains before, inevitably, he ends his time with Madrid. He is unpopular there. His moods and his methods are not classy enough for Real, and he somewhat brazenly used the media spotlight to audition for his next coaching job.

He does not deny that, by preference, he would prefer to return to England. His dearest wish would be to coach Manchester United, but even at 71 there is no inclination by Ferguson to vacate his seat, even for Mourinho.

The one person Ferguson would, in a heartbeat, take home with him from the Spanish capital would be his erstwhile pupil, Ronaldo. There was a hug, a father-and-son moment, at the end of the first game on Wednesday, and there will doubtless come another after the return match on March 5, no matter who wins.

The encounter is still where it was at the beginning: even. Both camps regard it as 50-50 after Ronaldo's goal had equalized an earlier strike by United's young forward, Danny Welbeck.

That, too, was a header, a fine one, a rehearsed one, but not comparable to Ronaldo's.

Welbeck knew exactly where Wayne Rooney would direct a corner kick because they practice it in training. Sergio Ramos kept tight to Welbeck, six yards from the goal, but when the United striker stepped a pace back, Ramos failed to go with him.

Up leaped Welbeck, and in went the ball.

The other game ended 2-2 in Donetsk. The best goal there was scored with both feet off the ground by Shakhtar's Brazilian Douglas Costa, but the final shot was a header from Dortmund's Mats Hummels three minutes from the end.

The pleasure was shrouded by the tragedy that preceded it.

CHAPTER 2

Reaching New Heights: Real Madrid

Real Madrid's multiple Champions League and Club World Cup titles over the past decade are a testament not only to Ronaldo's skills, but also to the skills of his teammates. With his move to Madrid in 2009, Ronaldo's reputation as a star athlete and celebrity grew. He was called the team's saving grace, scoring game-winning goals that compensated for his team's lackluster defense. However, Real Madrid has stars beyond Ronaldo. Their talent becomes crystal clear when Ronaldo is forced to face it himself, playing against them as part of the Portugal national team.

Madrid and Ronaldo Give Happiness a Chance

BY ROB HUGHES | SEPT. 19, 2012

MADRID — Real Madrid, whose history almost defines European Cup glory, was pushed to the limits of its talent and its competitive instinct to overcome Manchester City in the opening round of the Champions League.

"The DNA of my team is back," coach José Mourinho said late Tuesday, after Real came back twice from a goal down to defeat Manchester City, 3-2, at Bernabéu stadium in Madrid.

Mourinho's face was still flushed, his eyes still startled, and the trousers of his expensive suit no doubt permanently stained green where he slid on the grass at the final whistle. No matter. Victory — and relief — does this to a man under pressure to win, win, win.

Within seconds, a microphone was shoved toward him, and Mourinho blurted out: "We didn't deserve to suffer so much. The players proved to me that if they want, they can.

"If they want to be top professionals and if they want to respect Real Madrid's history, every match, not just against City or against Barcelona, every single match they can do it because last season they proved it," he said.

Close by, Cristiano Ronaldo was also on the turf. He had scored the last-minute winner, and, after being lifted by his teammate Marcelo, Ronaldo was being asked on television whether he was happier now. "This is not important," Ronaldo responded.

He has yet to explain, and may never explain, his sullen refusal to celebrate his previous goals for the team.

"What is important," Ronaldo said, "is the fans, and the three points. It doesn't matter if I'm happy or sad."

Maybe he is right. Maybe the melancholy of a man so gifted counts for nothing. And it is worth stating that in the match Tuesday he at times transcended each and every millionaire performer with his touch, his movement, his vision.

Well, almost every other. City's Yaya Touré was extraordinary, in a very different way, throughout the night.

Touré is a colossus in mind as well as in body. Four times in this contest, the 1.91-meter, or 6-foot-3, Ivorian surged out of his own half. It was like watching Usain Bolt turn on the afterburners and leave men in his wake.

The strength of Touré, the spirit that makes him believe he can run through three or four tackles as if they do not exist, is so exciting. Alas, when he did decide to part with the ball, his pass or his shot lacked accuracy.

Real Madrid, though, could not constrain him. Mourinho had tried by leaving out his more creative players Mesut Ozil, Luka Modric and Kaká, and packing his midfield with sturdier warriors like Michael Essien.

Finally, at 68 minutes, Touré got the pass right and paved the way for Edin Dzeko, City's first substitute of the game, to score with a cool, calm, low shot. Now, Mourinho had to react.

He exchanged the muscle of Essien and Sami Khedira for the flair of Ozil and Modric, and in attack he withdrew Gonzalo Higuaín and put on Karim Benzema.

Bingo. Ozil started the move that ended with Marcelo curling in the equalizer. But then City led again when Alexandar Kolarov's deceptive free kick sliced its way through the heavily defended goalmouth and beat goalkeeper Iker Casillas at the far post.

If Casillas was slow to read that shot, City goalie Joe Hart had been defying Ronaldo all night long with acrobatic stops. However, Hart was as deceived as Casillas had been when Benzema turned just inside the penalty box and sweetly timed a shot for the second equalizer.

Only three minutes to go, and had that been the concluding thrust it might have been a just result.

Real, and that man Ronaldo, would not settle for that.

In the 90th minute, the Portuguese attacker cut in from the left, and though his low, right-footed shot bore a hint of speculative striking, it had the element of surprise. Hart might have seen it late because his defenders were in his line of vision, but Ronaldo's game-winner bounced agonizingly close to the keeper's left hand.

It was over the line, the game was over, and so, apparently, was Ronaldo's attempt to convince the people that scoring makes him sad.

The guys who do suffer are goalkeepers, and Hart said sharply after the game: "You can't go 2-1 up with five minutes left and lose. It's not on. We have to blame ourselves, and don't expect me to say it's O.K. losing at a stadium like this. It's not."

The Champions League is back, and not just at the Bernabéu. In France, Paris Saint Germain's expensive new side routed Dynamo Kiev, 4-1, with Zlatan Ibrahimovic scoring a penalty that makes him the only man to have scored Champions League goals for six teams — Ajax, Juventus, Inter, Barcelona, A.C. Milan and now Paris.

The nomad scores wherever he goes. But when Málaga defeated Zenit St. Petersburg, 3-0, a local talent, the 20-year-old Isco, scored twice from midfield.

He looked very happy indeed to celebrate before the fans.

Spain Deserves Appreciation, Not Criticism

BY ROB HUGHES | JUNE 26, 2012

WARSAW — Spain is the best team in the world, and Portugal's Cristiano Ronaldo has looked on occasion to be the best player in the Euro 2012 tournament.

Still, as the two sides prepared to line up against each other in their semifinal Wednesday in Donetsk, Ukraine, negativity was all around.

The critics say tiki-taka, the Spanish policy of keeping the ball with short, accurate passing, is becoming a bore. And they say the new Spanish custom, of playing without a recognized central striker, is a tactic of fear by a team and a coach who are more intent on defending titles than expansively expressing its talents.

And when Cristiano Ronaldo delivers — as he did with three goals in the last two games, with truly outstanding performances that transcended his team — the skeptics counter that if only Ronaldo were less cocksure, less of an arrogant peacock.

Maybe the heat and the slow, long hauls between venues in the two host nations are getting to the critics. Maybe those who sit in TV studios or write in newspapers and on blogs — some of them former players — are unwilling to acknowledge that changed times, changed tactical thinking and changing personnel come with the territory.

As we move toward the final stages of this tournament, it is inevitable that players from the same top clubs find themselves on opposite sides when two countries meet. In the first Euro 2012 semifinal, Ronaldo will be directly opposed by four Real Madrid players who have been his friends, his support, his providers during the past two seasons as he has been on fire, scoring more than 100 goals for the club.

Now, they want to stop him. If he plays on the left, as he did so imperiously against the Czech Republic last Thursday, he is in direct opposition to the Real fullback Álvaro Arbeloa. If he drifts into the central role, from where he magnificently headed the winner against the Czechs, another Madrid defender, Sergio Ramos, will jump against him.

If he moves back to find space in the midfield, Real's Xabi Alonso will be at his heels.

And if he escapes them all and finds himself one-on-one against the goalkeeper, his club captain, Iker Casillas, will be the last, redoubtable, barrier between himself and a goal.

It was Real's defense — and Ronaldo's prowess in attack — that made the difference when Madrid finally stopped Barcelona from hogging the Spanish league. Now it is that defense, and some of Barça's tiki-taka midfield creators, who are out to stop him.

In any other circumstance, this might seem like too much of an emphasis on the individual. But, lest anyone forget, Ronaldo did eclipse his own national side last Thursday.

Sure, he needed the passes of João Moutinho, and Nani running down the other wing, and the solid defending from which Portugal sprang forward. And even though getting the ball to Ronaldo is such an obvious ploy for Portugal, he still has so far fired in more than 30 shots in four matches — far, far more than any other striker.

It is intriguing to hear his club mates speak of how they intend to reduce him to a normal presence in Donetsk. "Playing as a team is the best way to stop him," says Xabi. "Whatever people are saying, we are not going to change our way of playing. We'll try to cover for Arbeloa if he need help, and try to make sure Cristiano doesn't settle and isn't allowed to turn." Spain's defense — often overlooked because the team's emphasis on the midfield means that area has so much control that it is seldom vulnerable — just happens to be the most solid in this tournament, just as it was at the 2010 World Cup. It has conceded just one goal in four games here.

Spain coach Vicente Del Bosque, himself a magnificent defender for many years at Real Madrid, spoke of the obvious when he said, "If our defenders are good, then we will be closer to winning the tournament because we will always create a chance." Note the singularity of that comment. He said one chance, not many.

In this tournament, where the heat is sapping, especially in Ukraine, one goal and a clean defense is a winning formula. But when the critics lament Spain for lining up without a bona fide center-forward, they are old-school in their thinking.

They might as well criticize Barcelona, surely the most attractive club on earth, for choosing to play Lionel Messi as its notional central striker. Messi, of course, is Argentine and not eligible for this competition. But the guy is everywhere and anywhere when performing for Barcelona; not a fixed central striker, but nevertheless the scorer of 70 goals during last season alone.

Instead of criticizing Del Bosque, it might be wiser to acknowledge that without an obvious central attacker, his team has the best ratio of goals for and against in the tournament. Germany has scored nine goals, but conceded four. Spain has scored eight, conceding only one.

It must be doing something right. The argument over the "false No. 9" could be turned on its head. Injuries have deprived Spain of its record all-time scorer, David Villa, and Fernando Torres is still not the rampant scorer he once was.

So Del Bosque improvises. He leaves a hole at the focal point of his attack, trusting Cesc Fàbregas, Xabi, Andrés Iniesta or Xavi Hernández to infiltrate that space with insouciant runs from midfield. If you remember Xabi's header against France, or indeed the second goal that came when Pedro was fouled in the penalty area, both were classic "center forward" runs into the box.

It amounts to tactical innovation, to exploiting space and knowing how to get into scoring positions. It demands the effort, the timing, the opportunism of a striker, from players working hard in other areas. And they are harder to defend against if they are of no fixed, traditional roles.

What I suspect is happening is that critics are tired of Spain winning all the prizes. Tired of applauding it. Tired of the story never changing because the secret of success is repetition.

Flash of Red Leaves United Speechless

BY SAM BORDEN | MARCH 5, 2013

MANCHESTER, ENGLAND — Cristiano Ronaldo nudged the ball over the goal line from a sharp angle, then slid past the post and behind the net. As the small Real Madrid section of fans at Old Trafford roared, Ronaldo, who twirled his magic for Manchester United for six seasons before departing for Spain, held up his hands and asked for restraint.

It was, in many ways, surprising. After all, this was Ronaldo's first game at Old Trafford since he left United, and his goal with about 20 minutes remaining gave Madrid a 2-1 lead on the night, a 3-2 aggregate lead in the two-game series and essentially secured its passage to the Champions League quarterfinals. If ever there was a situation to celebrate, this would seem to be it.

But Ronaldo stayed calm, as if not wanting to rub it in on his former team. And on the sideline, his manager, José Mourinho, who memorably sprinted along the touchline after his team scored an important goal here nine years ago, stayed under control, too. For both, the reticence seemed a tacit acknowledgment of the bizarre and contentious circumstances that led to Real Madrid's victory.

Even Ronaldo acknowledged that he was not the story of the night. Neither was United Manager Alex Ferguson, who surprisingly left one of his top scorers, Wayne Rooney, out of the starting lineup. Instead, it was Cuneyt Cakir, a Turkish referee, who seized the spotlight in this hotly anticipated Round of 16 showdown with a startling decision to send off Manchester United midfielder Nani in the 56th minute. The decision left United to play the final half-hour with only 10 men.

Afterward, Ferguson was so enraged that he sent his assistant, Mike Phelan, to meet with members of the news media. Phelan laughed when asked if Ferguson had asked Cakir for an explanation. "I don't think the manager is in any state to speak to the official," Phelan said with a wan smile, adding that Ferguson was disturbed because he and the United players thought they had played a near-perfect game tactically before the red card.

Mourinho, speaking frankly, agreed. "In my opinion, the best team lost," he said simply, applauding United's play and criticizing his players for not responding until late in the match. Without the red card, United might well have won, Mourinho said.

Two years ago, Mourinho and Real Madrid were victimized by a similarly disputed red card when Pepe was sent off in a Champions League semifinal against Barcelona. This decision was equally harsh, Mourinho said, and he acknowledged that Cakir could have given Nani only a yellow card after he lunged in with his foot waist-high in an effort to play the ball away from Álvaro Arbeloa.

After the collision, both players rolled on the ground in apparent pain and Cakir reached for his pocket as he waited for Nani to get up. At that point, it seemed a yellow was coming.

But as United's trainers helped Nani to his feet, Cakir showed a red. Nani stopped short, staring at the official, who is highly regarded by the European association and worked a semifinal at last year's European Championships. A group of United players sprinted at Cakir, screaming in anger. Ferguson stormed down to the field from his seat on the bench, shouting and pointing.

Replays showed there was significant contact between Nani's foot and Arbeloa, but by rule, Cakir had to determine that Nani had endangered the safety of his opponent with the challenge. Simply being reckless should have brought a yellow, which was United's argument.

"The decision was amazing," Phelan said, shaking his head.

After Nani departed, the game unraveled quickly for United, which had stymied Real Madrid with a strong defensive effort and led by 1-0 on the night and by 2-1 on aggregate after a Sergio Ramos own-goal early in the second half. Ten minutes after Nani's red card, though, Luca Modric ripped a curving shot from about 25 yards, banking it into the net off the goal post to tie the score.

Three minutes later, Gonzalo Higuaín whipped in a cross that found Ronaldo, who had received a lengthy ovation from the United fans before the match to acknowledge his return. When he turned the ball into the net, however, the famed stadium went mostly silent as the goal all but ended United's hope of winning titles in both England and Europe.

"It was an emotional moment for me, for both games, but especially tonight," Ronaldo said in a television interview of facing his former club.

United fans surely will not feel similarly tongue-tied when it comes to Cakir, though the referee's decision took the focus off Ferguson's decision to drop Rooney from his lineup. Ferguson, the United manager since 1986, has a reputation for making unexpected choices, but leaving out Rooney will surely be remembered as one of his most provocative.

Rooney, 27, has been at United since 2004, and although he has been linked to the occasional transfer rumor — there were recent reports that Paris St.-Germain might be interested — Rooney has maintained that he is only interested in playing for the Red Devils. Match nights like these, he has said, are what he most enjoys.

On Tuesday, however, he was a substitute, leaving Robin Van Persie as the lone striker with the veteran Ryan Giggs, 39, who was making his 1,000th professional appearance, supporting him. Danny Welbeck, who scored in the first leg, joined Nani on the wings.

Rooney finally entered in the 73rd minute, and he helped United press for a miracle in the final moments. But Real Madrid goalkeeper Diego López was stout as Los Blancos — who are essentially out of the Spanish league title race — advanced to this tournament's final eight.

Of course, none of the players' performances will be remembered as much as that of Cakir, whose decision brought a stream of vitriol from the United players at the final whistle. Rio Ferdinand led a charge of United players who stamped after Cakir, with Ferdinand sarcastically applauding in the official's face before being led away by his teammates.

JOHN PETERS/MAN UTD VIA GETTY IMAGES

Cristiano Ronaldo of Real Madrid and Rafael da Silva of Manchester United in action during the UEFA Champions League Round of 16 second leg match between Manchester United and Real Madrid at Old Trafford on March 5, 2013 in Manchester.

Afterward, none of the United players spoke to reporters, reportedly on instructions from management. Ferguson also stayed away, remaining in a dressing room that Phelan described as "very distraught."

He added: "Playing Madrid with 11 men is very difficult. We feel very disappointed that we ended the game with 10 men."

A Top Performance Before the Clásico

BY ROB HUGHES | OCT. 23, 2014

LONDON — How would you deny, even if you wanted to, that Cristiano Ronaldo and Lionel Messi are the ultimate players in a global game?

It is wrong to talk about individuals transcending a team sport. Wrong, but it is as inevitable today as it used to be in the times of Pelé, Di Stéfano, Cruyff or Maradona.

Now, with Messi and Ronaldo, it is happening again.

The two players are headed for the first Clásico of the season on Saturday at Bernabéu Stadium, a game in which Luis Suárez could make his debut at some stage in Barcelona's front line after his four-month suspension for biting an opponent at the World Cup.

But ahead of that charged encounter in Madrid came the small but not inconsequential matter of Champions League soccer. Real Madrid holds that trophy. Barcelona wants to win it. And both had group games to play before they could even think of the Clásico.

On Tuesday, Messi set up Neymar to score at the Camp Nou against Ajax. Messi then struck the second goal before sitting out the final 20 minutes as a spectator on the bench.

On Wednesday, Ronaldo scored the first goal of his career at Liverpool's legendary Anfield Stadium. And, with Madrid beating Liverpool, 3-0, Ronaldo also was able to sit out the final 20 minutes.

He had an ice pack on his left knee but a smile on his face that told the world it was a purely precautionary measure. Ronaldo confirmed he would be ready for Saturday.

These are strange liberties that allow Barça and Real to rest their stars — their superstars — during Champions League games against former winners of the trophy. Ajax is no longer a mighty competitor because it relies too heavily upon producing young players who, sooner or later, are sold on the open market.

Liverpool is no longer a true competitor because despite spending twice the $100 million or so it received from Barcelona after selling them Suárez this summer, it has found that the Uruguayan striker is just about irreplaceable.

Mario Balotelli, one of the many new faces in Liverpool's team, was withdrawn after 45 forlorn and frustrating minutes during which he seemed disinclined to take on the work of being Liverpool's frontrunner. He possibly knew that his game was up and that he would not play another minute beyond halftime when he was seen exchanging jerseys in the tunnel with the Madrid defender Pepe.

Souvenirs at halftime is not the Liverpool way, not soccer's way.

The crowd of 44,000, all that Anfield can pack in until an expansion in the near future, had grown impatient waiting for "Super Mario" Balotelli to live up to his billing. Brendan Rodgers, the Liverpool coach who gambled on the Italian and spent tens of millions more trying to build a defense, said he would "deal with" the shirt-swapping incident behind closed doors.

Rodgers, however, knew on Wednesday that he was beaten by something special.

The coaches, Rodgers and Madrid's Carlo Ancelotti, exchanged knowing glances when Ronaldo struck midway through the first half. It was a collector's item, another extraordinary goal from Ronaldo's trove.

The Portuguese had never scored in five previous visits to Anfield. He put that to bed by initiating a pass-and-go interplay with James Rodríguez, the star of Colombia's fine showing at the World Cup. In such instances, Ronaldo does not give the ball; instead, he loans it to a colleague.

As Cristiano passed it sideways, he instantly made a move forward. As he glided between Liverpool's two central defenders, a top-class goal must have been forming in his mind.

Do the great players know in advance that, for example, Dejan Lovren would stretch and fail to intercept the delicately lobbed through ball from Rodríguez?

Did Ronaldo prey on that Lovren failure, and if he did, could he have known that Martin Skrtel, the other center back, would try to put his imposing frame between Ronaldo and the goal?

No time for thought, only for instinct. And Ronaldo simply watched the ball drop over his shoulder before he caught it and half-volleyed his goal beyond the goalkeeper Simon Mignolet.

Could Mignolet have saved it? Well yes, if he could have anticipated the audacity, the timing and the purity with which it was struck.

A silence momentarily came across the stadium.

Then, as Liverpudlians have done throughout time, the home fans cheered the majestic quality of a strike against their team. This, as much as the atmosphere when Liverpool men and women sing "You'll Never Walk Alone," is an intrinsic part of the club's heritage.

"I feel pleased and proud," said Ronaldo after being applauded off the field when his early exit was announced. "But what is important is the result. The spectators clapped Karim Benzema as well when he scored."

Indeed they did, twice. Benzema first rose to head Real's second goal, then preyed on pandemonium in the Liverpool defense. All three goals came before halftime. Liverpool was dispirited and defeated, and Madrid could start resting Ronaldo, Toni Kroos and Marcelo in a processional second half.

"I have the fortune to be manager of these players," Ancelotti said on television, with one eyebrow raised in that characteristic fashion of his. "Liverpool started with intensity. After 20 minutes we scored and started to play good football."

Before very long, Ronaldo, or Messi, will eclipse Raúl's all-time scoring record in the Champions League. Messi has 69, Ronaldo 70, and Raúl finished his career with 71.

Raúl was simply, if superlatively, a goal scorer (principally for Real). Messi and Ronaldo are so very much more — creative all-around players who border on genius.

A Victory for Haves (Real) vs. Have-Nots (Roma)

BY ROB HUGHES | FEB. 18, 2016

LONDON — Cristiano Ronaldo got a monkey off his back and most likely helped Real Madrid banish its lingering problem in the Champions League.

By striking the opening goal in Real's 2-0 victory at Roma on Wednesday, Ronaldo scored for the first time away from home since November. And with that goal and a later one from Jesé Rodríguez, Real Madrid moved comfortably toward beating an Italian opponent in the knockout stage of the Champions League for the first time since 1987.

Both goals were momentous. Ronaldo's 89 goals in the Champions League are more than any other player's. Jesé, who gets few opportunities to play for his boyhood team, notched his first goal in the Champions League.

The performance was far from classic, and Roma is a shadow of what it was in the past. Still, you could see what it meant in the way that Madrid Coach Zinedine Zidane walked onto the field to shake hands with each player at the end. Zidane, who played for five years with Juventus in Italy and then five years with Real, knows how much of a mental barrier a losing streak can be.

There is no comparison between what Real spends on players and what Roma can afford, but parity seemed to exist for almost an hour of sweat and toil on Wednesday. Two men, neither of them the biggest names on their teams, perhaps had the best performances of that hour.

Mohamed Salah, the Egyptian on Roma's right wing, kept sprinting past Madrid's Marcelo, almost as if the fullback was not there.

That in part is because Marcelo is a Brazilian left back, and playing fullback is not natural for most Brazilian players. Their adventures carry them forward, instead, as so-called wing backs.

Though Salah's speed is thrilling, he seldom provides an end product to his galloping runs. He knows how to burn his way past most men but not what to do with the ball when a decent crossing pass or shot is required.

Marcelo came closer than Salah to scoring when he linked up with Ronaldo and produced an audacious volley that looped over Roma goalkeeper Wojciech Szczesny, but the ball veered just wide.

It was the most exciting attempt of the first 57 minutes. But then, with Marcelo again on Ronaldo's wavelength, the stalemate was broken.

Marcelo passed the ball to Ronaldo, who suddenly cut inside the edge of the penalty box and turned Roma defender Alessandro Florenzi inside out. Florenzi tried throwing his body in the way of Ronaldo's shot, with the ball looping off the Italian defender and over the head of the keeper.

Madrid (and Ronaldo) could easily have scored twice more before Jesé struck. Jesé, who came on as a substitute, ran at a retreating defense down the right, slipped the ball between the legs of Lucas Digne and then buried his shot hard and low across the goal line.

The game was over for Roma, and the curse of Italian opponents lifted for Madrid. When the dust is settled after the return match in Madrid on March 8, it will all have seemed obvious.

Ronaldo is 31 and entering that phase where his greatest gift, his speed, will begin to fade, as will his physique and other marvelous skills. But for now, he still has it, attested by his 12 goals in the Champions League this season.

For Roma, its finest players — Francesco Totti, 39, and Daniele De Rossi, 32, — could manage appearances only as substitutes as they deal with injuries late in their careers.

As much as the wily Luciano Spalletti has tried to revive Roma in his second stint as coach, he has a team that has been cobbled together. No fewer than six of the players who started for Roma on Wednesday do not even belong to the Italian club.

The goalkeeper, Szezesny, is on loan from Arsenal. Salah is lent out from Chelsea. Digne belongs to Paris St.-Germain. Right back Antonio Rüdiger is owned by Stuttgart in Germany. Forward Stephan El Shaarawy is under contract to A.C. Milan.

Diego Perotti has just moved from Genoa. And striker Edin Dzeko made his move to Roma from Manchester City permanent after starting out on loan at the beginning of this season.

The deals cut both ways. Roma has 25 players out on loan or on shared contracts. It is a mighty reflection on how things have changed economically for Italian clubs, once able to buy almost any player they desired.

But Roma's roster is a shocking way for a team to operate in the Champions League, where the Real Madrids, the Barcelonas, the Manchester Citys, Chelseas and the Paris St.-Germains all run a surplus of highly talented and sought-after players. Those clubs are fielding teams in up to four competitions and need players in reserve.

But there is a discrepancy — a growing one — between teams that might actually win the Champions League and those who are just making up the numbers to fill out the tournament. Real Madrid's significant lead over Roma exemplifies that.

And Madrid is not even the favorite to land the European trophy. That would be either Barcelona or Bayern Munich, both of whom play in the competition next week.

Real Madrid Wins Ugly in an Un-Classic Barcelona Clásico

BY ROB HUGHES | APRIL 3, 2016

LONDON — "You don't get to choose when you lose," Barcelona Coach Luis Enrique said in the Camp Nou stadium. "We didn't experience the joy we were hoping for."

"I liked everything about my players," said his Real Madrid counterpart, Zinedine Zidane. "We've put in a massive effort, and when I see the whole team fighting for their teammates and for the coach, nothing is better."

It sounded like role reversal: Luis Enrique, a gritty competitor in his days as a player, lost for the first time in 40 games as coach. Zidane, who as a player was arguably the prime example of Real Madrid's "Galáctico" policy of loading up on high-priced stars, was extolling the pragmatic way to win.

Real's 2-1 win on Saturday in the Clásico was exactly that: pragmatism over beauty.

Madrid came from a goal and a man down to win in Barcelona after trailing for the first time since 1965. It avenged November's crushing 4-0 loss to Barcelona in Madrid. The decisive goal Saturday came moments after Madrid's captain, Sergio Ramos, got himself sent off for persistent reckless fouls.

Ramos's red card, if anything, seemed to spur Madrid to win the contest. Its goals from Karim Benzema and Cristiano Ronaldo had some beauty — Benzema with an improvised scissors kick in a crowded goalmouth, and Ronaldo with fine control of the ball off his chest and then a deadly finish with his right foot.

You could ask where the defense was during both of Madrid's scores, along with when Gerard Piqué struck Barcelona's only goal with a header following a corner kick earlier in the game.

You could question many things about the timing of the Clásico, which came right after two tough rounds of World Cup qualifiers for South American players and just before Barcelona's challenging Champions League match against Atlético Madrid on Tuesday.

And some might suggest that the whole atmosphere at the Camp Nou on Saturday was too distracting and too inevitably mawkish as the Catalans used the occasion to pay homage to Johan Cruyff, the former club great who died in Barcelona on March 24.

Thousands of Barcelona fans held up signs with the club's colors of burgundy, yellow and blue to form a mosaic that simply stated, "Gràcies Johan." Thanks for founding Barcelona's way of playing, a style that puts beauty to the forefront.

The word for thanks was pointedly spelled out in Catalan, not Castilian Spanish. An accompanying minute of silence for Cruyff was stained for many with tears.

Unfortunately, the game that followed was not allowed to be Cruyff-like.

Madrid, after its humiliation in November, came with its midfield defense stiffened by the presence of Casemiro, whose combative instincts were preferred over the scoring instincts of one of the club's current Galácticos, James Rodríguez.

Interestingly, Casemiro was not selected by Brazil to play against Paraguay or Uruguay in the week before the Clásico, nor was Madrid's left back, Marcelo. Six players for Barcelona — including the prolific front three of Lionel Messi, Luis Suárez and Neymar — played for their national teams in South America, returning to Spain barely 48 hours before the game.

In the first hour of this less-than-classic Clásico, Barcelona was on top, even though Messi flickered, Suárez fluffed a chance from seven yards out, and Neymar was fitful. Madrid let them have the ball and concentrated on blockading its third of the field.

While Madrid's play was nowhere near the brutal fashion of how José Mourinho used to instruct his players to kick the Catalans, Ramos did at times seem more intent at hacking away at Suárez than at the ball.

"Justice doesn't exist in football," was how the Barcelona defender Javier Mascherano — no shrinking violet himself — described the affair.

As it was, Barcelona seemed largely drained of energy and joy. Its attacking trident of Messi, Neymar and Suárez will need to be much fresher against Atlético than they were Saturday.

Messi did force Real's goalkeeper, Keylor Navas, to make a remarkable save as he clawed away a chipped shot. But after the opening goal, the last half hour turned Madrid's way.

Madrid equalized on a classic breakaway, with Benzema launching himself horizontal to the ground to volley the tying goal.

Gareth Bale then had what looked like a perfectly good headed goal disallowed for what the referee thought was a foul on Jordi Alba. Madrid, though, sensed that Barcelona was spent and went for the victory.

It came when Bale crossed the ball toward the far post. Dani Alves was there for Barcelona, but so was Ronaldo. It was no contest. Alves misjudged the flight and Ronaldo — taller, stronger and much, much better — was composed in bringing the ball down and unerring in his finish.

The two most expensive wingers in soccer, Bale and Ronaldo, had run miles to augment their team's defensive entrapment of Barcelona, but they still had the energy to win the game.

Give credit to Real Madrid. Credit to Zidane for eschewing the graceful way that personified him as a Galáctico and showing that, as a coach, he knows how to win ugly.

A tired and emotional Barcelona lost when its house was full of remembrance. But it remains six points clear atop the Spanish league, so the loss will have lasting effect only if this performance is repeated in the Champions League.

Real Madrid's Emergency Strategy: Leave It to Cristiano Ronaldo

BY ROB HUGHES | APRIL 13, 2016

LONDON — The word superstar is too loosely used today in regard to team games, but it is impossible to imagine Real Madrid getting out of the hole it had dug for itself in the Champions League without its brightest talent, Cristiano Ronaldo. After losing the first leg in Germany, 2-0, Real Madrid had to beat Wolfsburg by three clear goals Tuesday at Santiago Bernabéu stadium in Madrid. Ronaldo, looking like he had ESP, scored all three goals in Real's 3-0 victory.

Madrid is a flawed team that, like many other Real teams dating to the 1950s, relies upon exceptional individuals to win on any given night. Ronaldo is the latest continuation of that. Real needed three goals, and Ronaldo scored them.

Karim Benzema and Gareth Bale, superb players in their own right who cost more than $170 million combined to acquire, were the supporting cast. They played O.K. within the team context, but neither scored. None of Ronaldo's goals were anywhere close to a masterpiece. The first two were a matter of being in the right place at the right time, of sensing an opportunity and then reacting to a lack of concentration by the Wolfsburg defense. (The first goal also involved a lucky break, a ricochet off a defender's shin.)

But there he was, Johnny on the spot.

The decisive third goal was a free kick, but again, it was not a trademark Ronaldo strike of awesome beauty or power or timing. Ronaldo said that Real's goalkeeper, Keylor Navas, had spoken to him just before the free kick and suggested he surprise everyone by shooting it softly for once.

Ronaldo did just that, and, uncannily, two players in the defensive wall — Naldo and Josuha Guilavogui — parted just as the ball reached them, leaving a hole that deceived their own goalkeeper.

"It's mythical, magical," Sergio Ramos, the Madrid captain, told reporters after the game. "Cris is always important, he's our goal scorer, our icon.

"We don't need to flatter him any more," Ramos concluded. "He's a man who gives everything for the badge, and when he's on form, the team knows it."

That in itself defines the culture at Real Madrid. The current coach, Zinedine Zidane, was once able to conjure up majestic game-winning shots when he was a player, including his finest goal of all, which won the 2002 Champions League final in Glasgow.

That, too, was against a German opponent, Bayer Leverkusen. It was an imperious goal, a volley struck at hip height with the flawless technique of a great player.

The instinct that made him a great player may or may not make Zidane a great coach for Madrid, if he is given enough time. But can someone who has been there and done that in a similar situation be credited with knowing that the best plan Tuesday was to leave it all to Ronaldo?

Ronaldo is 31, an age when the body usually begins to slow, but the numbers indicate that the Portuguese star is anything but waning. In the Champions League alone this season — because it is so intrinsic to Real Madrid's history — Ronaldo has scored 16 times in 10 games. On Tuesday, he scored his third hat trick in the tournament this season as he increased his career tally in the event to 93 goals. In 129 Champions League games for Manchester United and for Real, Ronaldo has scored 63 goals with his right foot, 14 with his left foot and 16 with his head. His goal off the free kick was the 11th time he has done that in the competition.

Multiply all of that many times over and you have Ronaldo's career total of 482 goals in 665 games, with 359 goals coming in 342 appearances for Real Madrid.

Ronaldo repeated on Tuesday a mantra that he has been fond of lately: The stats, he said, do not lie. "Una noche perfecta," or one perfect night, said Ramos, looking across at Ronaldo, who had the game ball tucked inside the jersey like he was pregnant.

All of this tells us nothing about Real Madrid's strange season or its ability to advance and perhaps win an unprecedented 11th title in Europe's top club competition.

Like the Ronaldo who came before him (the Brazilian who played in Madrid from 2002 to 2007), Cristiano is a phenomenon. But how does a coach, particularly an inexperienced one like Zidane, build a reliable team plan around one player's extrasensory perception?

The plan worked handsomely on Tuesday. Ronaldo worked it, but the effort was not entirely solo because the team's defense, more compact in shape, was far more reliable than it was in Wolfsburg.

Yet there is a thought around the Bernabéu that this summer will be the time to offload Ronaldo. To sell him while his fame might still fetch a decent price. To reconstruct the team, to maybe liberate talents of its other stars, such as Bale.

It is all speculation. Nobody knows until Friday which opponent Madrid will face in the semifinals. And no one can say if Madrid's philosophy of acquiring star after star and throwing a bunch of them at a coach — any coach — can work in the modern game.

It failed in Wolfsburg last week, but it worked out quite well in Madrid on Tuesday.

All of us, if we are honest, have no idea what makes Ronaldo such a singularly extraordinary winner. His talents are many, and his attitude at times is that of a prima donna. But he delivers, with quite frightening regularity, the ability to destroy two game plans — both his team's and the opponent's.

Portugal vs. Wales Represents More Than Ronaldo Against Bale

BY ANDREW DAS | JULY 5, 2016

THE SCOREBOARD will read Portugal vs. Wales. The subtext will be Cristiano Ronaldo against Gareth Bale.

But do not be surprised if Wales Manager Chris Coleman is right, and the outcome of Wednesday's Euro 2016 semifinal is decided by someone else.

"At this level of international football, someone makes a wrong decision and within two or three seconds you are behind in the game," Coleman said.

He should know. Wales won its first game on a late goal and lost its second on a dagger of a score in second-half injury time. Sure, Bale leads his team with three goals, but the most memorable moments have been produced by others. Portugal, too, has learned that star power only goes so far; it has as many goals from Nani (two) as it does from Ronaldo.

That made it easier for Bale to play down his rivalry with Ronaldo, his Real Madrid teammate, ahead of the match. But then Bale, who supplanted Ronaldo as the world's most expensive player when he moved to Madrid, is having a better tournament and — from all outward signs — considerably more fun.

And the pressure will not be on Bale, or Wales, on Wednesday. Wales is playing in its first European Championship, and its run to the semifinals has been a thrill ride of late goals, lusty singing and postgame kickabouts with the kids (a tradition UEFA moved to end on Tuesday).

The Euros have been considerably more frustrating for Ronaldo and Portugal. Portugal did not win a game in the group stage, advancing only on the strength of two remarkable Ronaldo finishes against Hungary, and it waited 117 minutes to produce a shot on goal in its round of 16 match against Croatia. It won only after Ricardo Quaresma banged in the rebound of that shot, and then it needed penalties — including a clincher by Quaresma — to outlast Poland in the quarters.

Through it all, Ronaldo's frustration at his inability to take over games has manifested in a series of shouts, stomps and glares. But Portugal has experience — it has been to the semifinals in four of the past five Euros — and, for better or worse, it still has Ronaldo, who remains one of the world's best players and one with a knack for delivering in big moments. And Wednesday surely qualifies as one.

"The players all have the same goal, and it is not just about Cristiano and Bale," Portugal Manager Fernando Santos said Tuesday. "All players want to go as far as possible."

Reprise of '14 Final Has Repeat Result: Real Madrid Wins Championship

BY SAM BORDEN | MAY 28, 2016

MILAN — The ingredients were familiar. An early goal. A frenzied rally. A grueling stretch of extra time. A crushing finish.

Familiar, too, was the result: Real Madrid defeated Atlético Madrid in the Champions League final here Saturday night, beating its crosstown rival for the continental crown for the second time in three years.

Real Madrid has now won 11 European championships, a record total — and also 11 more than Atlético, which was agonizingly close to finally tasting glory.

For all the similarities to the 2014 final, though, this match at the San Siro stadium was not a rerun.

Last time, Real Madrid fell behind in the first half, scored in the dying seconds of added time and then ran away with a three-goal win in extra time. On this night, it was Real that scored early, Atlético that leveled the score late, and the Merengues, holding off Atlético's pushes, who barely edged to a victory, 5-3 in a penalty shootout, after a 1-1 draw.

The game ended, as so many of Real's seem to, with Cristiano Ronaldo shirtless. Ronaldo, who was largely quiet throughout the match while playing with what appeared to be a lingering leg injury, was given the opportunity to seal the win after Juanfran missed Atlético's fourth penalty kick. Injured or not, Ronaldo did not waver, coolly shooting the ball past goalkeeper Jan Oblak, ripping off his own shirt and waving it wildly as his teammates ran toward him.

Gareth Bale leapt in the air. Marcelo danced. Amid the celebration, Ronaldo found a moment to embrace his manager, Zinedine Zidane, a former star for the French national team who became the seventh man to have won a Champions League title as both a player and a coach.

"I had a vision," Ronaldo said, adding that he had asked Zidane if he could take the fifth penalty kick "because I was going to score the winning goal."

The Atlético players slumped in a heap near midfield. They were understandably battered, having come just seconds from winning the club's first European title two years ago only to make it back to the final and be gutted again.

Diego Simeone, Atlético's manager, looked dazed as he trudged around the field trying to console his players. He seemed to have made the right moves — his halftime substitute, Yannick Ferreira Carrasco, scored the tying goal with about 10 minutes remaining in regulation — but it was not enough.

Atlético slumbered through a somnolent first half but was far better in the second and looked more likely to win in regulation. After it could not, the team was left with regrets, most notably a missed penalty kick from Antoine Griezmann just after halftime that could have changed the tenor of the game. Shooting toward his team's fans, Griezmann bounced his shot off the crossbar as Simeone grimaced on the sideline.

"I don't believe in excuses," Simeone said. "To lose two finals is a failure. We must now go home and tend to our wounds."

Real Madrid's victory concluded a bizarre season — even by the club's circus standards — in which its president, Florentino Pérez, fired Manager Rafael Benítez in an attempt to shake the players out of an early-season slump. Pérez then elevated Zidane, who had been coaching Madrid's second team but had never coached in the top division, and watched as Zidane ripped through the next five months and became the eighth manager to claim the continental crown in his first season.

"When you have players of this caliber," Zidane said, "you can achieve something big like we have tonight."

This was the fourth European cup final to be played at the San Siro stadium, and it was similar to the last two editions, both of which had late-game drama. In 1970, Feyenoord, from the Netherlands, beat

Rangers, of Scotland, by 2-1 after extra time. Thirty-one years after that, Bayern Munich beat Valencia in a thrilling penalty shootout.

Those games were classics on their own, but Saturday's had a different feel, if only because of the geography involved. Two years ago, an estimated 90,000 Spanish fans traveled to Lisbon for the final — many of them in caravans that clogged the motorways — and while few expected a repeat of that number, the Spanish presence in the city center here was impossible to miss.

Spotless white jerseys. Red-and-white striped scarves. Countless Ronaldo shirts. A fair few for Fernando Torres.

A flock of Real Madrid fans sang, long and loud, down the street from the towering cathedral early in the morning; steps away, in the Galleria Vittorio Emanuele II, Atlético fans drowned out the noise of tourists and shoppers.

These clubs, and their fans, know each other so well that there was no novelty, no fascination to the meeting. It was simply another round between rivals that are separated by little more than a 20-minute taxi ride across the Spanish capital.

Not surprisingly, the game was played with an edge. Tacklers flew in early, and there was little early flow from either team as constant fouls bogged down play.

One of those fouls — Juanfran knocked over Bale about 15 minutes in — preceded a goal by Real Madrid's Sergio Ramos. With the free kick off to the right flank, Toni Kroos whipped in a cross, and Bale flicked the ball with his head before Ramos slid in and jammed it over the line. Ramos took off running, celebrating the goal, his first in the Champions League since his last-second header sent the 2014 final in Lisbon into extra time.

The Real fans roared while the Atlético fans fumed, their frustration turning to anger after they saw replays of the goal: Ramos appeared onside for Kroos's free kick but offside for Bale's flick; the goal should have been ruled out.

Of course, it was not. And just as Atlético did two years ago, Real

MATTHIAS HANGST/GETTY IMAGES

Cristiano Ronaldo of Real Madrid lifts the Champions League trophy after the UEFA Champions League Final match between Real Madrid and Club Atlético de Madrid at Stadio Giuseppe Meazza on May 28, 2016 in Milan.

fell into a shell after its opening strike, soaking up pressure and nearly making it to the finish line with a 1-0 victory before a late goal changed the story.

This time, it was Carrasco. Oblak made a dazzling save to deny Ronaldo at one end, and seconds later at the other, Juanfran sent a cross in front of the goal that was there to be finished.

Carrasco ran to the stands to kiss his girlfriend. The red-and-white-striped end of the San Siro erupted.

At that moment, it felt as if Atlético might go on and finish what it could not two years ago. Things felt different.

But they were not. The ending was just the same.

Real Madrid, Hard to Define, Firms Its Stamp on Champions League

BY RORY SMITH | JUNE 3, 2017

CARDIFF, WALES — Real Madrid's original Galácticos, that glittering collection of talent, could not do it. Neither could the Dream Team that Johan Cruyff built in Barcelona in the 1990s, nor its spiritual heir, constructed by Pep Guardiola and fueled by Lionel Messi, two decades later.

Several iterations of Bayern Munich, Juventus, Manchester United and A.C. Milan, teams regarded as among the best of their age, of this age, fell short only narrowly, but fall short they did. Louis van Gaal's Ajax came closer than most, only to see glory snatched away by penalties.

For the first 25 years after the European Cup morphed into the Champions League, nobody was able to retain the title. It had come to be seen as the final frontier, soccer's ultimate honor, the feat that would separate the immortal from the merely great.

On Saturday here in Cardiff, the current incarnation of Real Madrid at last broke through the barrier.

This Real Madrid did not need to win another Champions League to have its place in history. It had already won two of the last three editions of the competition, beating its fierce rival, Atlético Madrid, in Lisbon in 2014 and again, on penalties, in Milan last year.

But in sweeping past Juventus, 4-1, on Saturday, thanks to two goals from Cristiano Ronaldo and one each from Casemiro and Marco Asensio, the team turned its recent primacy into something more lasting, something approaching hegemony. In time, this will be remembered as Real Madrid's era.

The nature of the era, though, seems harder to discern. Those teams that live longest in soccer's communal memory tend to define, or be defined by, something — their legacy endures partly because of what they come to represent. They offer a blueprint that others might, in their own way, follow. They do not simply conquer the game. They change it, too.

Trying to pinpoint the meaning of this Real Madrid team, though, is to grasp at smoke. Recently, the academic Steven G. Mandis published a book called "The Real Madrid Way." It purported to extrapolate the values that led to the team's relentless success.

It caught many in Europe, particularly within soccer, by surprise. There appears, after all, to be no overarching philosophy deployed by Florentino Pérez, the club's president, to build a team, and no style of play that Zinedine Zidane, its coach, has instilled in his players. On the surface, its success offers no lessons.

Indeed, it can seem to be quite the opposite. Real Madrid is the antithesis of much of modern soccer's dominant thinking. This is an age in which concept is king. Soccer craves those coaches who see themselves as representatives of some higher idea, and it lionizes teams that claim to have discovered a revolutionary system, whether on the field or in the transfer market.

Real — almost alone now — scorns it all. The best example is the player who scored the crucial second goal in Cardiff, the one that broke Juventus's spirit and drained its resolve: Casemiro, a generally unspectacular Brazilian defensive midfielder, but the sort beloved of coaches searching for balance on a team.

If Pérez had his way, Casemiro would not play. The Real president, in fact, once advised Rafael Benítez, Zidane's predecessor, to exclude him from a vital Clásico against Barcelona. His thinking was simple: Casemiro does not sell enough jerseys and rarely brings the fans to their feet, so he cannot be especially important. Real was duly beaten, and Benítez eventually fired. One of Zidane's first acts was to bring Casemiro back to the team.

At first glance, then, it would be easy to assume that Real Madrid's victories do not stand for something more, do not represent some greater truth. They are not victories for a belief or a system. They are simply victories for Real Madrid, and that is all that Real Madrid cares about.

That is not to say they are unwarranted. Juventus started with a blistering urgency on Saturday, but over the course of the match, Real's superiority shone through. Ronaldo's first goal came against the run of play and was canceled out by Mario Mandzukic's wonderful overhead kick.

The three that followed in a flurry in the second half, though, were a fair reflection of Real's dominance, Zidane's team flicking through the gears, finding an acceleration and a ruthlessness that Juventus, the Italian champion, could not match. Juventus's defense, its pride and joy, a grizzled, hard-boiled unit that had seemed able to stifle any opponent, was torn apart, time and again, almost at will.

It would be inaccurate, and foolhardy, to pretend that this was the product of nothing more than good fortune, or to dismiss all that Real has achieved since 2014 as some sort of oddity, one that defies logic and explanation. This is not a team that should be denied credit for the greatness it has earned simply because it does not fit within today's narrow definition of what greatness looks like.

This Real Madrid does stand for something. It stands for a simplicity that jars at a time when soccer is in thrall to complexity; for the cold truth that if you put 11 extremely talented players on a field, they are capable of remarkable things; that if you gather enough excellence together, it concentrates, ferments, becomes exponentially more potent — capable of overcoming any hurdle at all. It represents the fact that at heart, when the miasma of theorizing and extrapolating and intellectualizing clears, soccer is a simple equation, one in which the team with the best players generally wins.

It is not something another team can replicate, a lesson that can be learned or a pattern that can be mimicked, which is why it is so often ignored. It is something that is really only available to a team of the wealth, power and history of Real Madrid.

But that does not make it any less valid, or any less worthy of praise. There is a Real Madrid way, which does not need a book to define it. The Real Madrid way is to win. That is how this era will be defined, in hindsight: as the era in which Real Madrid won, and won again, and won again. There is no way it would rather be remembered.

CHAPTER 3

National Identity: Playing for Portugal

Cristiano Ronaldo's fame is a source of pride in his home country. In addition to playing club soccer for Manchester United and Real Madrid, Ronaldo is a member of the Portugal national team. He made his debut on the team in 2003 and played for them in the 2004 European Football Championship. He became captain of the team in 2008 and has appeared in 147 games, more than any other player in the team's history. He led the team to victory in the 2016 European Championship, winning the Silver Boot award as the Championship's second-highest goalscorer in the process.

After Slump, Ronaldo's Goals Come in Bunches

BY JERÉ LONGMAN | JUNE 17, 2012

KIEV, UKRAINE — Cristiano Ronaldo once compared goal scoring to ketchup in a bottle. Sometimes, as much as you try, it won't come out. Then it pours out all at once.

In Portugal's first two matches at the European Championships, Ronaldo had accumulated no goals, only unrelenting criticism and taunting comparisons to Lionel Messi. The complaints were familiar: Ronaldo's individual skill, however impressive, could not transform a team. He came up small in the big competitions. He was petulant, self-absorbed, the incredible sulk.

But the ketchup analogy seemed apt Sunday as Ronaldo scored twice in a 2-1 victory over the Netherlands in Kharkiv, Ukraine, sending the Dutch home stunningly early and advancing the Portuguese to the quarterfinals against the Czech Republic. More goals might have gushed forth, but Ronaldo twice hit the post. And he willingly involved his teammates, not just himself.

Meanwhile, the Netherlands fittingly wore black on a night that turned funereal. It needed a two-goal victory, as well as a Denmark defeat by Germany, to advance. Germany won, 2-1, and will face Greece. But two years after finishing second at the World Cup, the Dutch crumbled at Euro 2012, scoring two goals in three games, fissuring internally and mustering a defense that was even more feeble than its attack.

"Ronaldo got so much criticism in the last game, and he is back now," Bert van Marwijk, the Dutch coach, told reporters. "That is how fast things can change."

On Sunday, the Netherlands had no choice but to attack. So van Marwijk did what many had been urging him to do: he started Klaas-Jan Huntelaar, the leading scorer in the Bundesliga, up front in a 4-2-3-1 formation and sat the defensive midfielder Mark van Bommel for the more creative Rafael van der Vaart.

The plan was desperate, but it also seemed inspired in the 11th minute. Arjen Robben slashed inside from the right wing, creating space and passing softly to van der Vaart, who curled a wonderful shot inside the left post. The Dutch had a 1-0 lead and hungered for more.

It was a redemptive moment for Robben, who has had an awful month. He missed a penalty kick in extra time for Bayern Munich in an eventual defeat to Chelsea in the Champions League final. Days later, during an exhibition, Bayern fans jeered him. In February, the Bayern legend Franz Beckenbauer had called Robben selfish.

If anyone could commiserate, it was Ronaldo.

He pouted as Portugal lost its Euro opener to Germany, 1-0, then stripped off his captain's armband and headed for the dressing room while his teammates applauded their fans. He missed two inviting shots in the next match, against Denmark, as his team won, 3-2, despite him. Danish fans began taunting Ronaldo with chants of "Messi, Messi, Messi."

This past season, Ronaldo scored 60 goals for Real Madrid, which wrestled the Spanish league title from Barcelona, but Messi scored 73 goals, a European record. It is Ronaldo's chafing misfortune to be considered only the second best player in the world, to be great but always in the shadow of his rival.

At a news conference the other day, Ronaldo snapped that, a year ago, Messi was exiting the Copa América prematurely in his native Argentina.

"I think that is worse," Ronaldo said.

It was a peevish comment. And it only invited more ridicule that, for the Portuguese national team, Ronaldo has often been flamboyant but hollow, like one of his ostentatious step-over moves.

That perception began to change in the 28th minute Sunday. After a Dutch giveaway, Ronaldo sprinted onto a pass from Joáo Pereira with impeccable timing and a clinical finish to equalize at 1-1. Maarten Stekelenburg could only wave a futile hand in goal as the Dutch began to wave goodbye to their chances.

Ronaldo was now emboldened, audacious. He rocketed a shot from 35 yards with such force that Stekelenburg's parry flew beyond the penalty area. Diving to the ground on a corner kick, Ronaldo headed another shot wide before halftime. He had the predatory sense of a fighter whose opponent was weak and sagging on the ropes.

In the second half, the Dutch became more frantic to score, needing at least two goals, and also became more vulnerable. In the 74th minute, Ronaldo struck again on a breakaway. He ran onto a diagonal pass from Nani, cut into the penalty area, corkscrewed defender Gregory van der Wiel into the turf, then calmly put the ball inside the left post.

SERGEI SUPINSKY/AFP/GETTYIMAGES

Portuguese forward Cristiano Ronaldo celebrates after scoring his second goal during the Euro 2012 football championships match Portugal vs. Netherlands on June 17, 2012 at the Metalist stadium in Kharkiv, Ukraine.

His team up, 2-1, Ronaldo slid on his knees and pounded his chest. At the final whistle, he sat on the ground and shook his fists. If he could still be childlike, it was now in exuberance instead of petulance.

Without Ronaldo, No Chance at All

BY ROB HUGHES | JUNE 28, 2012

REDUCING A GOOD team's participation in a tournament to the penalty shoot-out is a painful enough exercise in any circumstance. But it seemed particularly perverse that Portugal should go out of the European Championship without Cristiano Ronaldo, its best finisher by far, not even stepping up to take one of the penalty kicks.

He stood, he waited, he was wasted. It was like appointing a man to be king, and not letting him try on the crown.

Let us be straight: The Iberian neighbors had slugged out a sterile stalemate in the hothouse of Donetsk, where the stadium was not even full. (Perhaps as a consequence of uncompromising attempts to rip off fans with high prices across Ukraine for everything short of breathing this tournament?)

Maybe the Spaniards and Portuguese who did not make the long trip to Ukraine's most easterly city in this tournament had an inkling of what would come. Maybe they knew that the talk that Portugal would try to attack Spain and not try to suffocate their skills, as others did, was hogwash.

In the end, after 120 minutes without a goal, the turkey shoot was inevitable, if soulless.

It came for two reasons. Ronaldo, who had transcended his teammates in earlier games against the Dutch and against the Czechs, could not be such a free spirit against a Spanish side that knew his tricks so well. Four players on the Spanish side are his teammates on Real Madrid, while others from Barcelona have played Ronaldo a dozen times since he joined the Spanish giant in 2009.

Portugal needed other players to stand up to the plate, and none could. Portugal's coach, Paulo Bento, said he was terribly proud of his men for their strength in defense and their energy in the counterattacks. However, when the best opening came on a break approaching the 90th minute, it was Ronaldo who squandered it.

Time was running out when Raul Meireles burst through from the center circle. Spain's defense was outnumbered as Meireles arrived in the penalty box. He could have taken responsibility to shoot, or he could pass to Ronaldo.

Meireles did what Portugal has done throughout this tournament: He passed to the best player on his team. However, Ronaldo was off balance, and not for the first time in this semifinal, he shot too hastily, mistiming his kick with the left foot. The ball squirmed high and wide.

The talisman for Portugal was tired. Others had been withdrawn, including Spain's great playmaker, Xavi Hernández. But in some ways, the Spanish coach Vicente Del Bosque regretted changing his mind, changing his game plan and changing his lineup.

Del Bosque listened to the critics who think they know better than the coach of the world's best team of the past four years. He abandoned his so-called "False No.9" style by putting in the big Sevilla striker, Álvaro Negredo.

Negredo, and not Fernando Torres, who as Del Bosque said, has had his chances and failed to score. Negredo, rather than Fernando Llorente, the Basque who has come along to this Euro simply for the ride.

Negredo looked like a lumbering man who was out of synch with the quickness and mobility of the Barça and Real Madrid players, so after 54 minutes he was withdrawn. Cesc Fàbregas, another midfielder but one with a better instinct for getting into scoring situations, came on.

That altered the balance of the contest, but it did not break the stalemate.

However, Fàbregas would get to be the winner of the lottery. During those penalty kicks between players who know each other too well — because the best of the Portuguese play in Spain's league — it was fascinating to see Ronaldo whisper in the ear of his goalie, Rui Patrício.

Ronaldo could tell Patrício which way Xabi Alonso and Sergio

Ramos would place their penalties because Ronaldo trains with them throughout the year at Madrid. The advice might have contributed to Patricio's diving to save Xabi's kick, but Ramos had a more cunning plan: he waited for the goalkeeper to commit to a movement, and shot the other side.

And, with Real's Iker Casillas in the other goal, this insider knowledge did bring a peculiar intrigue to the shoot-out. The ultimate chapter of that penalty drama never happened.

It was meant to be Casillas versus Ronaldo, teammates at Madrid and opposing captains of their countries. But somebody had to gamble on when Ronaldo would take a penalty. It was decided, between Ronaldo and the coach, that he should be the fifth in the sequence — the tenth in the shootout, as it turned out, with Spain electing to be first on each kick.

"I was going to take the fifth penalty," Ronaldo later explained. "It was just a question of me speaking with the coach. He said 'Do you want to take the fifth one?' and I said 'Yes.' Sometimes I take the first, the second or the third. I agreed to take the fifth, but we missed two."

In fairness, Casillas saved the first shot from João Moutinho, and then Bruno Alves shot the fourth Portuguese penalty over the crossbar. Ronaldo, the man with all the answers in other games, was left staring to the sky, seemingly asking why he was forsaken.

He chose wrong, his coach chose wrong, and they ended up hurting only themselves. Portugal's futility was the image of Ronaldo standing idle while others played and missed.

Ronaldo's Latest Masterpiece Puts Portugal in Semifinals

BY ROB HUGHES | JUNE 21, 2012

WARSAW — Cristiano Ronaldo is playing with such high levels of invention, bravery and desire that he is carrying Portugal in the European Championships.

The tournament's first quarterfinal pitted the Czech Republic against Portugal on Thursday. At least that was what it said on the team sheets. The reality is that two men transcended the rest.

One, Ronaldo, was a conjuring artist at high speed. The other, goalkeeper Petr Cech, used every inch of his 6-foot-5 frame to twist like a corkscrew, diving right and left, high and low to deny Ronaldo.

Two of Ronaldo's shots struck the post after beating Cech. Finally, after 79 minutes of this duel, the Portuguese captain defeated the Czech captain with a header of such force and direction that the ball carried into the net even though Cech got a glove on it.

Portugal advanced to the semifinals with a 1-0 victory, though the final score could have read: Ronaldo 1, Czech Republic 0. Portugal will play Spain or France in the semifinals in Donetsk, Ukraine, on Wednesday.

Seldom has one country owed so much to one man. Seldom has a single player transcended the others on the pitch to the point that he seemed to defeat the notion that soccer is first and foremost about the team.

On Sunday, Ronaldo scored the two goals against the Netherlands that gave Portugal the victory that put it in the quarterfinals. In Warsaw on Thursday, beneath the closed roof of Poland's national stadium and with a crowd urging on the Czechs, it seemed to be Ronaldo against everybody.

At times, four opponents were trying to shackle him. The fans were against him because they desperately wanted the Czech Republic, the last of the Eastern European teams in the competition, to reach the semifinals.

The Czechs ran themselves to exhaustion, but they were an ordinary team against a better opponent.

Thursday's game featured two moments of classic Ronaldo. The first, after 26 minutes, demonstrated the bodily power he possesses as he came hip to hip with the muscular defender Michal Kadlec. Ronaldo shrugged him to the turf and drew a splendid save from Cech, the Chelsea goalie who knows Ronaldo from his Manchester United days. Cech got off his line quickly and smothered Ronaldo's shot with both hands.

That was the only save either goalkeeper made in the first 45 minutes, but as halftime neared Ronaldo applied more pressure. Raul Meireles picked out Ronaldo lurking between defenders in the penalty area. He took the pass down on his chest, then controlled it with one dab of his right foot as he turned too quickly for Kadlec to his right. Before David Limbersky could get within kicking distance to Ronaldo's left, the Portuguese captain whipped a shot with his right foot. The shot was beyond Cech, but it cannoned off the post.

The coup de grâce came later. João Moutinho had sped down the right flank and delivered a cross high to the far post. Ronaldo rose, rippling with power and desire to get past the nearest defender. His forehead made perfect contact, driving the ball down into the grass and back up on the bounce, through the grasp of Cech.

Ronaldo has drawn fierce criticism over the years from those who say he is a diva who does not deliver. The results tell a different story. He has delivered for Manchester United and Real Madrid, and he is certainly delivering now for his country on one of his sport's biggest stages.

Despite a Hex, Ronaldo Works Magic

BY JERÉ LONGMAN | JUNE 22, 2014

MANAUS, BRAZIL — The World Cup arrives every four years, and without fail it brings a good and possibly even true story about a witch doctor.

This particular witch doctor put a curse on the knees of Cristiano Ronaldo in February. These are not just any knees. The reigning world player of the year, Ronaldo is so agile and elusive that he is the only man known to have dated Kim Kardashian without marrying her for a reality show.

And this was no random application of the dark arts. The witch doctor happened to be from Ghana, which, like the United States and Germany, was drawn into the same group as Ronaldo and Portugal.

The spell involved something about four dogs, a special spirit and a whammy so potent it could not be cured by medical science, television evangelists or juice therapy.

"They can never see what is causing the injury because it is spiritual," Nana Kwaku Bonsam, whose name translates as Devil of Wednesday, told a Ghanaian radio station, Angel FM. "Today, it is his knee; tomorrow, it is his thigh; next day, it is something else."

Really, if you're going to be a witch doctor, you couldn't have a better name than Devil of Wednesday, although one wonders why Dr. Devil is giving interviews to an outfit named Angel FM.

Scoff if you will, but Ronaldo seemed to arrive in Brazil with the knees of an aging N.F.L. lineman. Tendinitis in his left knee, to be specific.

His own doctor told a Portuguese newspaper that the injury could threaten Ronaldo's career. The doctor suggested that Ronaldo take two months off. Ronaldo suggested that no one flies off to South Beach in the middle of the World Cup.

At training Friday, Ronaldo wore what was described as a brace on his ailing knee. Still, the Americans never doubted he would play on Sunday. This is soccer, after all, where players are writhing in agony one second and doing the Riverdance the next, having been magically sprayed with WD-40 and oven cleaner.

Plus, Portugal lost its opener, 4-0, to Germany. And four other players were already absent Sunday because of suspension and injury. Paulo Bento, Portugal's coach, put his team's situation in dire terms: "Either we win or we start packing our suitcase."

So you're thinking, wow, you have 23 players and only one suitcase? Talk about traveling light. But we move on.

Even a hobbled Ronaldo would be dangerous, warned Tim Howard, the American goalkeeper who joined Manchester United of the Premier League along with Ronaldo in 2003. Howard knows as well as anyone that Ronaldo is not all hair gel, preening good looks and six-pack abs.

"He's the single hardest working player I've ever been around, on and off the field," Howard said.

And that was just a reference to eyebrow plucking.

Not to mention, Howard added, that Ronaldo is big and strong and fast with impeccable control; gymnastic balance; a heavy, dipping shot and unmatched skill at getting the ball to heel, sit and roll over like a dachshund.

On Sunday, the Americans started five midfielders, trying to enhance their possession and cut off the supply to Ronaldo. To get in his way, to jostle him at times. To bottle him up the way children bottle fireflies.

"He never really got into a rhythm," the defender Matt Besler said.

And yet there was a risk in focusing on Ronaldo and ignoring others.

"If we pay too much attention to Ronaldo, someone else will beat us," Howard said beforehand.

In the fifth minute, his caution became prophetic as Nani, Portugal's other wing, pounced on an awkward clearance by Geoff Cameron. Portugal 1, United States 0.

Portugal, too, sought to avoid a desperate reliance on Ronaldo. He scored all four of the team's goals in a two-legged playoff victory over Sweden to qualify for the World Cup. And he led Real Madrid to its 10th European championship. But to think Portugal could defeat the United States solely on a gilded performance by Ronaldo, Bento said, would be a "terrible mistake."

"I would never put on his shoulders the responsibility of solving our problems," Bento said.

On Sunday, Ronaldo wore an apparent lightning bolt shaved into his head and a long-sleeved jersey, suggesting he was immune to the heat and humidity of the Amazon. His first pass wandered out of bounds. Then he brought the crowd alive with flamboyant dribbling, making the ball stop and start as if it were a student driver with a manual transmission.

Still, he did not seem fully fit or comfortable. He showed frustration at his lack of touches in the first half, bounced a long shot to Howard and ballooned a free kick over the crossbar.

At halftime, Ronaldo changed to a short-sleeved jersey. If he felt cooler, he was still not sharp. He bore in on Howard from the right flank but shot wide and ran his hand through his hair in annoyance. Soon, Jermaine Jones curled a blast inside the far post for the United States, and the game was tied at 1-1.

Portugal was frantic now for a win. But crosses to Ronaldo were thwarted repeatedly. Then Clint Dempsey chested home what seemed to be the winner for the Americans.

Jurgen Klinsmann, the confident American coach, had talked of his respect for Ronaldo and his desire to put him in his place. Until the final 39 seconds, the plan seemed to work. But Ronaldo needed only a moment to show his resilience and sense of drama.

Five minutes into added time, Michael Bradley lost the ball. On the counterattack, Ronaldo curved a perfect cross from the right flank. Silvestre Varela headed it home to rescue a 2-2 draw for Portugal. Howard could only put his hands on his head.

“Football’s cruel sometimes,” he said.

Hope is thin, but Portugal is still alive. Ghana remains, and the witch doctor must conjure another potion.

Still Waiting to See Cristiano Ronaldo's Brilliance

BY ROB HUGHES | JULY 5, 2016

LONDON — Will the real Cristiano Ronaldo stand up for his country? Portugal is possibly two games away from winning a major tournament for the first time. Ronaldo is its leader, its inspiration and its record-holder in every way you could measure a player.

Forget, for a moment, the media comparisons between Ronaldo and his Real Madrid teammate, Gareth Bale. They will meet on opposing sides when Portugal plays Wales in the European Championships semifinal in Lyon, France, on Wednesday.

But while Bale is enjoying a wonderful Euros so far and is handling reporters' questions with quiet eloquence on behalf of his team, Ronaldo is comparatively silent. Perhaps he is saving his statement for the field at the Stade de Lyon.

We have seen just 12 minutes of Ronaldo's best during the tournament — when he scored with a heel-kick against Hungary, then when he later soared to head a second goal in that group-phase game.

The goals were extraordinary examples from one of the most accomplished and athletic finishers of this or any other era. The backheel score, when he did not even appear to take a glance at the target, was simply audacious. The header seemed — again — to demonstrate that Ronaldo can, at times, defy the laws of physics.

He rose earlier and higher than any defender. He hovered in the air like a hummingbird. He waited for the ball and then met it with such force and direction that the goalkeeper stood no chance of saving it.

And looking at Ronaldo's face, you just knew that he did not doubt for a second that he was going to score both of those goals.

This, after all, is the player whose hat trick against Sweden singlehandedly qualified Portugal for this event in the first place. We might remind ourselves that no man is a team, but Ronaldo has defied that concept time and time again.

Just look back to the 2012 Euros, when Portugal played the Czech Republic in Warsaw. It was Ronaldo versus the Czech goalkeeper Petr Cech for at least an hour of that contest, with Ronaldo shooting, heading, dribbling, running, and Cech stretching this way and that to frustrate him.

So Ronaldo soared higher still and won the game with a header that was not that different from the one against Hungary in this year's tournament.

Yet take away those 12 minutes, and it has not been remotely vintage Ronaldo in this year's Euros. It has been painful to watch his petulance after Portugal was held to a scoreless draw by Iceland; his irritation as he threw a Portuguese television journalist's microphone into a river; and his glowering looks of disapproval when teammates failed to feed him pinpoint passes.

He has missed a penalty kick and not even come close to breaking his streak of failing to score on the 36 free kicks he has attempted at World Cups or European Championships.

But while he is there, while he is on the field, his fellow Portuguese will look to serve him. It is reminiscent of the way that Italian teams of a bygone era seemed to pass the ball for Luigi Riva even after the great striker was no longer on the team. And it is reminiscent of how the Swedes waited for Zlatan Ibrahimovic at this year's tournament, then exited without Ibrahimovic's registering a single goal.

Ibrahimovic came and went from these Euros with barely a trace of his presence, then signed a contract with Manchester United that will make him one of the highest-paid players around.

Ibrahimovic is 34, and according to him, his physical condition astounded the United doctors who assessed him last week.

Ronaldo is 31 and would doubtless surpass any medical screening made on him. He recently eclipsed Luís Figo's record of appearances for Portugal. And with 60 goals in 131 games, Ronaldo is far and away his country's top scorer. (Pauleta is second with 47 goals, and the legendary Eusébio scored 41 in just 64 games).

But, no doubt, Ronaldo is the star that his own private museum on the Portuguese island of Madeira shows him to be. "Cristiano is an example, as captain, of the spirit of this team," Portugal Coach Fernando Santos said Monday. "He wants to do well, and he wants to win. In this aspect, he has been fantastic. He's an example of what the team is."

Is he? One wonders if there is anything physical holding him back, or if the effort of helping Real Madrid win yet another Champions League title in May drained him. Yet Bale shared in that triumph, and he has looked energetic and full of self-sacrifice for Wales.

Do Portugal's tactics — setting out to nullify the opponents rather than imposing a style of its own — dull Ronaldo? He is by nature a peacock, showing us what he's got. But Portugal's focus at the Euros has been on avoiding losses, and they are willing to go through, if necessary, on penalty shootouts.

Ronaldo, for now, is relatively silent. His brooding, his stares at colleagues and his unpleasant disparaging of Icelanders who dared to frustrate him are blights on his talent.

The Portuguese, for so long a nation that would play beautiful soccer and then lose at the penultimate stage, are going about it in a different manner this time. Even with so decorated a leader, they are prepared to be as sterile as is necessary to squeeze out a trophy.

And love him or loathe his childish behavior, Ronaldo is the catalyst.

Portugal Beats Wales at Euro 2016 and Gets Another Shot at Glory

BY SAM BORDEN | JULY 6, 2016

LYON, FRANCE — The ball soared in front of the goal and Cristiano Ronaldo jumped, his body hanging in the air for what felt like one beat, two beats, three beats, four. His chest was pitched. His back was arched. His eyes were forward, locked on the target.

Then, just as a Slinky hops down a staircase — its coils bending in one direction before whipping forward over the threshold — Ronaldo simply unspooled.

The contact was flawless. A sweetly struck free kick or a long, dipping drive has poetry, but there is nothing quite like the way a ball compresses when it rebounds from a man's skull. Ronaldo snapped his neck, and the ball, as if it had engines attached, whizzed past the goalkeeper and rippled the net. The Wales defenders, beaten, dropped their heads. Ronaldo, gleaming, took off running.

It was a sumptuous goal on a largely bland evening, but it was the opening that was needed. Portugal, led by Ronaldo, its enigmatic captain, secured a place in the final of the European Championships with a 2-0 victory over Wales on Wednesday at the Stade des Lumieres. The Portuguese will face either France or Germany on Sunday at the Stade de France just outside Paris.

Ronaldo, who tied Michel Platini's record of nine career goals in the Euros, will now have another chance to deliver a first major tournament trophy to Portugal, 12 years after he and his teammates lost in the final of the 2004 Euros. For Wales and its superstar, Gareth Bale, the loss was an agonizing end to a surprising run that has captivated a nation and beyond.

"The players are gutted," Wales Manager Chris Coleman said. "It still hurts."

Even with the sting still fresh, Coleman and his players know this tournament was an incredible success. Wales was playing in its first Euros and its first major tournament since the 1958 World Cup. It had many players on its team who play for second- or third-division club teams. It began the competition in a group with England, Russia and Slovakia but made it to the knockout rounds, where it beat Northern Ireland and then upset Belgium in the quarterfinals to reach the final four.

No one could argue that Wales's run was anything less than remarkable. For Portugal, however, the scale was different, and winning this match meant something else. Portugal's players celebrated at the final whistle, but there were no histrionics or wild dances. Portugal has made it to at least the quarterfinals of every Euros since 1996, and this was their third semifinal appearance in that span, all strong performances that ultimately ended without a trophy.

"We haven't won anything yet," Ronaldo said. "We still have the dream."

The hype for Wednesday's match started early. From the moment Wales completed its victory over Belgium, Bale was hounded by the news media about facing Ronaldo, his Real Madrid teammate, in the semifinal.

"It's not about two players," Bale said more than once. "It is about two nations in a semifinal, 11 men against 11 men."

Bale was right, though it was also not exactly the 11 men that both coaches would have wanted. Wales was missing Aaron Ramsey, the team's spark plug who was suspended because of an accumulation of yellow cards. Portugal was without Pepe, a top defender, who sustained an injury in training.

Those absences, as well as the gravity of the occasion, led to a cautious — some neutral observers might even say dreary — opening half. There were few significant chances for both teams, and the pace of play was slow and sloppy.

This was not altogether surprising for Portugal, which had been inconsistent for much of the tournament. Portugal arrived at this stage having failed to win a game in 90 minutes — three group stage draws, an extra-time victory and a win on penalty kicks carried them — so there was no guarantee anything would change.

Ronaldo, too, had struggled to find his rhythm. There were moments of wonder — such as when Ronaldo scored two goals against Hungary — where he showed the skills that have perpetually put him in the conversation, along with Lionel Messi, about who is the best soccer player in the world. But there were also long stretches of inefficiency and pouting, when it felt as if Ronaldo had vanished.

Yet the Portuguese buzzed after halftime and Ronaldo, who changed from long sleeves to short at the break, was everywhere. First he rose high, a full head or two above defender James Chester, to head in the first goal in the 50th minute. Then he stalked the ball as it bounced away from the penalty area, shot it back toward goal and watched as his longtime teammate Nani redirected the ball into the net to give Portugal plenty of cushion.

"It was a strange feeling," Nani said. "It came out of the blue. It was mostly instinct."

Wales did its best to push back into the game over the final half-hour, but without Ramsey — and with Bale finally showing signs of fatigue — there was little hope. Bale tried a long shot that the goalkeeper blocked away. Ashley Williams blasted one that hit his own man. Bale laced another free kick that slammed into the wall of Portugal defenders.

There was no collapse from Wales — their fans, who chanted long and loud, would not allow it — but Portugal was stout. Wales, finally, ran out of time.

"We've given everything," Bale said. "We have no regrets."

Ronaldo will only hope that he can say the same after Sunday. Twelve years ago, he was just 19 when Portugal lost the European

Championships final to Greece, the underdogs, by a score of 1-0. It was a brutal, bitter defeat and, after the final whistle, Ronaldo wept on the field.

Now 31, he has already envisioned a similar ending, but with a twist.

"I hope that by Sunday," he said, "you'll be able to see me cry tears of joy."

Cristiano Ronaldo, Quiet Superstar, Can Win Portugal's Heart With Euros Title

BY SAM BORDEN | JULY 9, 2016

PARIS — Cristiano Ronaldo spends a lot of time alone. Alone on the wing, alone in his kitchen, alone in his thoughts, where, by his own admission, much of his focus is on whether he will again win the Ballon d'Or award — the world player-of-the-year honor, which, of course, is for a single, solitary superstar.

Ronaldo does not mind this (or, at least, he says he embraces it). Even by modern athletic standards, his entourage is necessarily small: his agent, his manager, a few close friends and his family. That is it. He often eats lunch by himself, often drives to practice by himself. Over the last 13 years, he has cultivated an image as someone who lives lavishly and luxuriously — estimates are that he is worth $320 million and so the pictures of him on a yacht are to be expected — yet also in relative quiet.

He has his 6-year-old son, Cristiano Jr. He has his agent and father or brother figure, Jorge Mendes. He has his soccer and his stardom and, depending on the particular parameters of the argument, his place on or near the top of the list of soccer's greatest figures.

But here is the thing: Much of Ronaldo's life is built upon his place at his club team, Real Madrid. This is not to say that Real Madrid is a house of loners or that there is no team spirit there; to the contrary, the club is strong and rich, and many of its supporters are passionate and devoted and true. But it is also undeniable that because of Madrid's exorbitant resources — last year's payroll was estimated at $180 million — there is a culture of stars, many of whom come and go. And Ronaldo, who has been the rare mainstay, is the brightest.

SAMUEL ARANDA FOR THE NEW YORK TIMES

Children training in Funchal, Portugal.

With Portugal's national team, though, it is different. Ronaldo is still the biggest star, even more so than with Madrid, but the meaning of his presence, and the results, are not the same. On Sunday, Ronaldo will captain Portugal when it faces France in the final of the European Championships, the first time Portugal has been in a major final since it was stunned, on home soil, by Greece in the 2004 Euros.

Ronaldo was 19 then, a wunderkind who cried on the field after the final whistle. It was a brutal, bitter experience, but it did not stick to him, did not tarnish him. Neither did disappointing defeats in the semifinals of the 2006 World Cup or the 2012 Euros. In this era, results in international play are an additive to a player's legacy, a bonus. Consider: Ronaldo and Lionel Messi are the near-universal choices as the best players in the game, yet neither has helped his country lift a significant trophy.

On Sunday at the Stade de France, that may change. Ronaldo has said, many times, that he craves a title for Portugal, that it is a dream for him. It is, presumably, a pure one, too: Winning will do little for Ronaldo financially. It will not make him more famous, either. Portugal has a population of a little more than 10 million; Ronaldo has six times that many Instagram followers.

What it would do, however, is bind Ronaldo to a group. It would bring him together, forever, with his teammates, with the support staff, with the coach, Fernando Santos, who watched Portugal lose to Greece while serving as a radio commentator and now, more than a decade later, has brought his country back to the cusp again. At Real Madrid, Ronaldo's winning the club's 10th (and 11th) Champions League title or its umpteenth Spanish league title does not come with a similar immortality. The team's dominance makes any one squad's glory bleed together with the rest. With Portugal, there is nowhere else for the color to run.

It is sometimes difficult to know whether Ronaldo actually wants that kind of collectiveness. In a recent documentary about him (titled, simply, "Ronaldo"), he describes himself as "an isolated person" and, in explaining why he played in the 2014 World Cup for Portugal despite being injured, says: "If we had two or three Cristiano Ronaldos in the team, I would feel more comfortable. But we don't."

Similarly, in an interview with GQ published this year, Ronaldo was asked to name the most important game of his career. After a moment's pause, he said, "When I score five goals."

Many athletes would have immediately pivoted the question to the team, to the fate of the unit. After Antoine Griezmann scored both goals in France's semifinal victory over Germany, his first response to a question included a lengthy ode to the team's training staff and equipment crew for their contributions. And a few seconds after Ronaldo's first response, he did relent and cite the Champions League final victories. But his initial reaction was telling.

Such an answer does not mean he is selfish or self-absorbed (though one could argue that the life-size wax figure and museum devoted to his personal history do). Instead, it may simply show just how little experience Ronaldo has with being part of a group.

At this tournament, Portugal has had the expected mix. Younger players, like midfielders João Mário and Renato Sanches, have shown poise and promise, while veterans, like Nani and Pepe, have offered balance and steadiness. Portugal did not impress for much of the last month — three draws in the group stage followed by an extra-time victory, a win in a penalty shootout and, finally, a solid defeat of Wales in the semifinals — but it did enough. Along the way, even as others contributed, many of the key moments, including the decisive goal against the Welsh, came from Ronaldo.

If he, and his teammates, can do it one more time Sunday, it will be a seminal moment for Portugal and its fans, as well as for Ronaldo, who, for a change, would not go down in history alone. He and his teammates would be celebrated together, praised together, lionized together. Most important, they would be remembered together.

So will he be giving something to them, or will they be giving something to him? In this case, it feels as if it would be a little of both.

At Euro 2016 Final, Portugal Loses Ronaldo but Defeats France

BY SAM BORDEN | JULY 10, 2016

ST.-DENIS, FRANCE — Cristiano Ronaldo was crying, his chest heaving, his knee throbbing, his heart aching like never before. Ronaldo, prone on the turf, sat up slowly and did what he surely never imagined having to do in a game like this: He wrapped his captain's armband around a teammate as his eyes clouded over. Then he lay back, shimmied onto a stretcher and was carried to the locker room.

That moment, just 24 minutes into the final of the European Championships at the Stade de France, felt critical. One of the biggest stars in the sport going off after less than half an hour? It was the sort of twist that can — that should — define an entire match. And it did.

Portugal, faced with the loss of its leader and its motor and its man who is always in lights, did not wither or wilt or wobble. Instead, the Portuguese dug in, carried the match into extra time and — with Ronaldo hobbling up and down the sideline — stunned France with a goal in the 109th minute, beating the hosts, 1-0, to claim Portugal's first major soccer trophy.

"We said we would win it for him," Pepe, the Portuguese defender, said of Ronaldo. Pepe grinned. "And we just managed to win it for him."

They did, though it was far from pretty. Portugal's run at this tournament was strange: It tied all three of its preliminary-round games, finishing in third place in its group (behind Hungary and Iceland), but in this first Euros of 24 teams, it qualified for the round of 16 anyway.

Then, after a late goal by Iceland in its final group game shunted Portugal to the opposite side of the draw away from juggernauts like Italy, Spain, England, France and Germany, it edged past Croatia in extra time, beat Poland in a nervy penalty shootout and knocked off Wales in the semifinals — its only win in regulation of the tournament — before pulling off the shocker on Sunday.

Critics will say Portugal was far from entertaining. The team led for only 73 minutes of the 720 it played at this event, but the results were undeniable. Even without Ronaldo, Portugal never faltered.

"It defies description; it could be a Hollywood movie," Portugal's José Fonte said afterward. "We've written our names down in history."

At the final whistle, while Portugal's players piled on one another in celebration, the French players sank to the turf. For a country still recovering from the terrorist attacks last November and enduring nationwide flooding as well as constant worker strikes, the Euros were seen as a chance to celebrate something grand together. To smile.

In the end, there was, perhaps, a surface satisfaction: The tournament was run smoothly, security was largely effective and there were no major incidents, but the lingering feeling for the French will be the disappointment of falling just short.

France had plenty of chances on Sunday, too, including one at the end of regulation when André-Pierre Gignac hit the post. Yet there was no precision, no bite, as France showed in its semifinal victory over Germany. Antoine Griezmann, who was France's star and scored a tournament-high six goals over the last month, struggled to make an impact and missed an open header from 6 yards out with his best chance of the game.

"Football can be very cruel," France's captain, Hugo Lloris, said. "The overriding emotion is a lot of sadness."

Adding to that was most likely the notion that this was an opportunity missed because of the void left by Ronaldo, who was barely on the field at all. Just eight minutes into the match, France's Dimitri Payet poked the ball away from him with one foot while Payet's trailing leg crashed into the side of Ronaldo's left knee.

Ronaldo crumpled immediately. No foul was called, and few players from Portugal protested, but the damage was clear. Ronaldo received treatment and tried to return to the field but went down again a few minutes later. Then, after another discussion with the trainers (and with his leg wrapped), he tried to play once more before, ultimately, sinking to the ground a final time.

Twelve years ago, Ronaldo cried on the field after Portugal was shocked by Greece, 1-0, in the final of its own home Euros in Lisbon. Ever since, he had spoken of trying to deliver to Portugal that long-craved glory, and having finally reached the precipice again, he broke down once it was clear that he would not be able to see it through.

"It was unfortunate," Ronaldo said. "But I always believed that these players, together with the coach's strategy, would be strong enough."

They were. Fernando Santos, the Portugal coach, took over the team in 2014, and after losing his first match in charge to France, in this stadium in an exhibition, Santos told the players that their goal should be to return here for this final.

That statement stuck. And even once Ronaldo exited, Santos made all the right decisions, shifting Portugal's formation to stifle France's attack and, later, bringing on Éder — a forward who is often criticized for inconsistent play — who delivered the title-winning goal.

With France pushing forward to try to score in extra time, there was an opening for Portugal, and Éder slid to his right just outside the penalty area. With a sliver of space, he unleashed a wicked shot from about 25 yards out that whizzed past Lloris's hand and rippled the net in front of the Portuguese fans.

"We knew we could surprise them at any moment," Éder said. "So that's what we did."

The final 10 minutes were frantic. Ronaldo, who returned to the bench in sneakers and a bulky knee brace just before extra time, waved his arms and shouted at his teammates as the seconds ticked away. Once the celebrations began, Nani, the vice captain, ran up to him and returned the captain's armband as Ronaldo welled up again.

The French trudged up to receive their silver medals. The Portuguese fans never stopped singing. Ronaldo joined his teammates on the dais and, gingerly, stepped to the front to raise the trophy as fireworks and streamers and sparklers lit up the night.

Then the Portuguese players returned to the field and gathered for a team photo. Ronaldo shuffled to the center and sprawled out in front. Hours earlier, he had lain nearby, tears running down his cheeks. This time, as the flashbulbs flickered and the trophy gleamed, he lay back again with his face aglow.

CHAPTER 4

Ronaldo Versus Messi

Cristiano Ronaldo and Lionel Messi are opposites. Ronaldo is six feet two inches tall, while Messi is five feet seven inches. Ronaldo is polished and model-like, while Messi appears unkempt. Ronaldo's playing style and personality are theatrical, while Messi is reserved. But despite these differences, the two soccer stars have achieved similar success. Both have won five Ballon d'Or awards, often score over 50 goals per season, and have scored over 600 goals in their careers. There is much debate about who is the greatest contemporary player, with strong arguments made for both sides.

Genius Has Company in Messi and Ronaldo

BY ROB HUGHES | NOV. 16, 2010

LONDON — Lionel Messi and Cristiano Ronaldo are the modern gods of a game played in every land on the planet.

They are young. They are living the dream. They are still exploring their limitations. And because they are growing as performers, we do not yet know their place among the greats.

But in one aspect they are already up there. They transcend the league in which they play. Barely a match goes by in which they fail to pull off a trick that makes watching them a joy. But beyond that, they actually outscore the goal scorers on their teams.

You would have to go back 50 years, to Alfredo di Stéfano's time at Real Madrid, to find such a phenomenon.

Di Stéfano was the playmaker, the conductor of Real's orchestra. And because of his ego, because he could do it, he matched, or almost matched, one of the sport's most extraordinary strikers — Ferenc Puskas.

More than that, they are scoring, and creating, winning goals.

Messi is the quiet one, Ronaldo the showman. Messi stands chin-high to Ronaldo. He is a manikin to an Adonis, a Mini to a Maserati.

Their fitness willing, we may get a direct comparison when Messi and Barcelona play Ronaldo and Real Madrid on Nov. 29 at the Camp Nou.

But statisticians are all over them every week.

The mania for stats can blur the beauty of their game. Seeing Messi dart between the tackles or Ronaldo glide so swiftly and powerfully through them is preferable to counting the notches on their belts.

The statisticians do not even agree on which of all the tournaments they play — La Liga, the Champions League, the Spanish Cup, the Super Cup, the Club World Cup and so on — they should include in their charts.

But let's settle on a number of seasons that make comparison worthwhile.

Messi, now 23, has been at Barça since puberty. He has grown up in the style of the club, and he knew even before he grew into the first team exactly how, where and when Xavi Hernández would make the passes or Andrés Iniesta would run for the ball or make decoy runs.

The maturing of Messi, from a 16-year-old debutant to something approaching the finished article, has been one consistent, upward spiral. Since Pep Guardiola, a former captain of the team, became the coach two years ago, Messi has come in from the wing to be the main forward.

He is free to move where instinct, skill and determination take him. He once played apprentice to Ronaldinho, then he dovetailed with

Samuel Eto'o, then for a season with Zlatan Ibrahimovic. Now Villa is his main accomplice in attack.

In 69 appearances under Guardiola, Messi has scored 66 goals.

Some of them were acts of great beauty and impudence, some the merest tap-ins. Beyond that, look at the 21 assists, or final passes, Messi has made.

That adds up to 87 goals scored or created by one player in 69 matches.

Ronaldo's chart over the same period is 46 goals and 13 assists in 52 games. But Ronaldo, 25, is Real Madrid's main penalty-taker. He is also perhaps the world's most accomplished striker of free kicks. His timing of kicking a static ball, his ability to impart swerve and spin as if by remote control, is better than David Beckham's.

And remember that Ronaldo has switched clubs — and switched cultures — twice. As a boy, he was schooled by Sporting Lisbon, and as a teenager, he was nurtured under Alex Ferguson at Manchester United. Now, having chosen to play for Real Madrid, he is under his second coach in his second year there.

The new coach, José Mourinho, makes different demands on the players than his predecessor, Manuel Pellegrini. A year ago, Ronaldo would have been granted more license to follow his whim.

That is because Mourinho — who like Ronaldo is Portuguese — is much stricter on methodology. He will let Ronaldo's gifts breathe, but within a framework that makes the team more solid, more defense-minded.

I doubt we will ever see Mourinho's Madrid leave just two defenders back, the rest all going forward, as Barcelona did against Villarreal last Saturday.

Guardiola explained that this was possible only if everyone on the team was prepared to work.

"It's not a secret," he said. "It is hard work, not just with the ball, but without it. Messi is the first one to run. The team follows him. They want to play in the pit of the opera, and it's not necessary for the coach to say they have to run to win the ball. They feel it."

It starts with Messi because it is ingrained in the players who come through La Masia, the academy: Pass and move. Run for the ball. Run with the ball. Run into spaces where your colleagues can find you with the ball.

There are statistics that show every player's role in this. Computers work out every meter a player runs, every beat of his heart, every ounce of energy expended. But don't fall for them. Facts and figures will never replace the thrill of seeing Messi or Ronaldo do the unexpected. We should use the word sparingly, but it's called genius.

Messi and Ronaldo: 2 Stars in Their Own Universe

BY ROB HUGHES | OCT. 8, 2012

LONDON — "It should be prohibited to say which is the best player in the world. They are both from another planet."

So said José Mourinho late Sunday after El Clásico, arguably the greatest game on this planet, ended Barcelona 2, Real Madrid 2.

To give it another perspective: It was Lionel Messi 2, Cristiano Ronaldo 2.

What is so extraordinary about these two individuals is that they transcend the team sport — and do so time and time again.

It isn't simply a case of counting their goals. If that were the attraction, then we must include Radamel Falcao, the Colombian now matching them goal for goal in the Spanish league. Falcao doesn't have a collection of fine creators around him, as Messi and Ronaldo certainly do.

The Colombian fires goals — steals them, really — for Atlético Madrid, which sells its star strikers on an annual basis to stay afloat financially.

Yet, Atlético now shares first place in La Liga with Barcelona. Falcao is so coveted by English clubs that he could be gone early next year. But he showed his instinct, his predatory gift to sense space and opportunity twice against fourth-place Málaga on Sunday.

First, he sped between two markers to strike from a corner kick. Second, again with two men on him, he "scored" what was listed as an own goal, off a defender whose legs appeared tied together as he attempted to deny Falcao. Atlético won, 2-1.

Nobody won at the Camp Nou. Nobody except the 99,786 people in the stands and the estimated 400 million who tuned in, as Mourinho observed, from time zones all around the world.

We all won, just as soon as we disregarded the Catalan choruses in the stands expounding separatist ideals against Madrid rule. We all won when we concentrated on planet soccer.

Back on this earth, Messi's team and Ronaldo's team showed the contrasting styles that can still make this the "Beautiful Game."

Mourinho hasn't always allowed this at the Camp Nou. Despite learning his trade as a coaching assistant with Barcelona, he has in the past instructed his teams to go there to destroy.

Sunday was different. Sunday suggested that the players now at his command are too good, and too proud, to be ordered to play negatively or to harm their fellow pros on Barça's side. They think they are better than that, and on Sunday, Real Madrid was marginally the better team.

Imagine the self-esteem required to step into this soccer citadel, listening to all but the 660 travelling Madrid fans, singing their anthem and roaring pro-Catalan slogans all night long.

But silencing the opposition with talent is a skill built into the ego that is Ronaldo. He yearns, whatever Mourinho says, to be the winner of the Ballon d'Or, to be recognized as the No.1 soccer player on earth.

Maybe this will be his year, because, with Messi and Ronaldo scoring virtually every game, what Ronaldo did during Euro 2012 was at times sensational. He outshone even Andrea Pirlo, the marvel of Italy, and Xavi Hernández and Andrés Iniesta, who stroked Spain to the European title.

Xavi and Iniesta were again in fine form for Barça on Sunday. So too were Mesut Ozil and Xabi Alonso for Madrid.

They would enhance any team. But when it came to the decisive actions, only two men scored on this field.

First was Ronaldo. Little was seen of him until the 23rd minute when, thanks to Karim Benzema's controlled turn and pass, the Portuguese struck.

He was given space because the right-sided defender, Daniel Alves, was out of position. It is easy to blame Alves, who is sometimes too Brazilian and freewheeling for his own good, but this time he was drawn to the center, trying to help out in an area where the home team was lacking, with Carles Puyol and Gerard Piqué injured.

The speed that which Ronaldo's brain can assess the situation is exceptional, as is his ability to take just a few strides and then shoot low, left-footed inside the near post.

Where, and when, would Messi retaliate? The very question reduces the team game to individuality, but the answer came within seven minutes. Like Ronaldo, Messi preyed on a defensive lapse.

The Argentine was alert, waiting almost, when Real's big defender, Pepe, misjudged an attempted header to clear. The ball fell, as so often it seems to do, to Messi, who flicked it beyond goalkeeper Iker Casillas faster than anyone could shout, "Watch out, Messi's about."

Madrid recovered. Its counterattacking style, so very different from Barcelona's plan to create rhythm through movement and short passing, created the greater chances, two of them squandered by Benzema.

Then, on the hour, Messi again conjured the ball into the net. He was felled by Alonso to the right of the penalty box. He struck the free kick so that it spun over the defensive wall, dipped down and swerved gracefully beyond the reach of Casillas.

Ronaldo, though, had to respond. He attempted an audacious overhead volley, injured a shoulder when he landed, winced, and within minutes ran through the pain when Özil split the defense with a low pass that Ronaldo finished in cool style.

All four goals — and Falcao's, too — were from the left foot. The two outstanding players in the Clásico truly are from a field "from another planet."

Ronaldo and Messi Reign in Spain

BY ROB HUGHES | OCT. 24, 2011

LONDON — The Cristiano Ronaldo crisis is over.

The Real Madrid star had never gone away, his form had been just fine, but because he was creating chances for others rather than scoring goals himself, the critics were asking, what is wrong with Ronaldo?

A hat trick inside 15 minutes against Málaga on Saturday evening put paid to all that. His first goal was a simple, predatory use of the instep to Ángel Di María's fine pass. His second was pure Ronaldo: a movement of his feet and hips that created the space by sending an experienced Argentine national team player, Martín Demichelis, into the wrong orbit, and then a sharp, low shot. And the third, following a corner kick when you would think Málaga would mark him as top priority, involved Ronaldo leaping and stretching with the agility of a limbo dancer.

All done and dusted before halftime. With Gonzalo Higuaín also scoring, Real had destroyed Málaga on its own La Rosaleda field. And though Málaga fought spiritedly in the second half, though its Qatari owner had spent millions of euros buying up new players this year, the result ended where it stood when Ronaldo finished his hat trick, 4-0.

One man, they say, never makes a team. But one man, if his name is Ronaldo, cost more than the sum of the players thus far recruited by Málaga.

"I'm happy with my goals," Ronaldo said after the game. "But what's really important is that we win, with or without my goals. We had a fantastic first half, probably the best minutes we've played this season."

Only one team, and one man, could be expected to top that.

Barcelona, the Spanish and European champion, kicked off after Madrid's work was done down in Málaga. But, shock, horror, Barça did not win in its own Camp Nou stadium.

It was held, 0-0, by Sevilla. Denied by a defensive cohesion that was masterful to behold. Nine men in that committed Sevilla defense put their bodies in the line of all Barça's firepower, and the goalie, Javi Varas, gave the performance of his lifetime, blocking Messi, Andrés Iniesta, Xavi and the rest with virtually every part of his anatomy.

Varas even stopped a penalty in injury time from Lionel Messi.

So the game ended 0-0, Madrid ended the night a point ahead of Barça in the league standings, and Ronaldo and Messi are tied with 10 goals apiece with eight games played in the season.

But how healthy, people ask, can it be for a whole league, one of the world's best, to be so fixated around two teams, and two particular superstars? The answer could be stood on its head. How remarkable is this duel, this exhibition of ego and excellence, that two men sustain week after week, season after season? I personally have seen enough soccer around the world to last a lifetime.

In more than 40 years, I have never seen two individuals who rise so often to display skills under pressure. They are conjurors of performance, they are blessed with fitness that sustains them when some opponents do everything legal, and more, to try to stop them.

Nobody believes the claim by Ronaldo that it doesn't matter if he doesn't score. The Portuguese has amassed more than 100 goals at the rate of one every game since he transferred from Manchester United to the Bernabéu. And when he went a month since his last scores — another hat trick in September — he clearly was peeved at not being the main man.

Why should we expect great players not to have egos? Peacocks do not display their feathers out of modesty.

But it is not a bad night in the stadium just because one of them does not get on the score sheet. Messi was not out of sorts or off form during Barcelona's stalemate against Sevilla.

His passes were still exquisite. His desire was phenomenal. His nemesis was Varas. Here was a goalkeeper, largely unheralded until now. At least 12 times, Varas got a hand, a leg, a shoe or a shoulder in the way of Barcelona shots and headers. Yet Varas was not even a full-time player when he was 23.

He was a goalie, but an amateur one, in Seville, his home province. Sevilla then took him on, but as a long-term understudy to its splendidly reliable keeper, Andrés Palop. Midway through last season, Palop, then 37, began to give way to Varas and then, in an era of such top-quality Spanish goalkeepers, the understudy became the king at age 29.

So, in a sense, you wanted him to save Messi's penalty late into the night in Barcelona. His dive to the left, his anticipation of where the Argentine would kick the ball, low inside the post, deserved it. However, the circumstances surrounding that penalty kick and that save were less sporting. It was a definite penalty because the Sevilla defender Federico Fazio tackled late and kicked the trailing leg of Andrés Iniesta in a clear scoring position.

The referee, in fact, was lenient in not showing Fazio the red card.

But Sevilla then sullied its own commendable night by cheating. Frederic Kanouté, who had been on the field for the last 23 minutes as a substitute, was yellow carded for dissent. Kanouté's response was added petulance. He walked up, kicked the ball away from the spot where Messi was waiting to take the penalty, then remonstrated in front of Messi. Still not finished, Kanouté then became embroiled in argument with Cesc Fàbregas and ended up red-carded for pushing or slapping Fàbregas in the face. The long delay, the unsportsmanlike attempt to disrupt the penalty taker, might have worked.

Messi's kick was tame. The famed left foot struck it at a height that was favorable to Varas. And the keeper moved fast to turn the ball around the post, to preserve a point that he and his team deserved, even with their last disputatious deed.

Sometimes, it is not all about the greatest stars of the sport. Sometimes a massed defense has a nobility and a just cause of its own. And we know, don't we, that another day, another game, Messi will score another hat trick that no goalie, however inspired, will prevent.

Champions League Final May Settle Ronaldo-Messi Debate

BY JERÉ LONGMAN | MAY 26, 2009

ROME — The debate has been raging since the Champions League final was set, so it was hardly unexpected Tuesday when a reporter asked Sir Alex Ferguson, the Manchester United manager, whether his forward Cristiano Ronaldo or Barcelona's Lionel Messi was the best soccer player in the world.

Ferguson asked whether the news conference query should be repeated in Ronaldo's native Portuguese. Ronaldo smiled and motioned at his manager, as if to say just hurry up and answer in English. Everybody else in the world seemed to have an opinion. Ronaldo wanted to hear Ferguson's.

"They are two fantastic footballers, both with the ability and courage to attack defenders all the time," Ferguson said diplomatically. "No matter how many times they get tackled, they get up and want the ball. Physically, they are different, but at the end of the day, how can you divide them? It's very difficult."

The outcome Wednesday of the premier European club competition could go a long way toward settling the issue, at least for now. Giddy anticipation promises soccer that will be artful and elegant, and the Ronaldo-Messi debate will serve as a kind of game within the game.

Messi, 21, a native of Argentina, has often been called the next Diego Maradona, but he has never enjoyed those comparisons to his wondrous and troubled countryman. Yet neither has Messi shrunk from the pressure of expectation.

In March, Maradona, now the Argentine national team coach, awarded Messi his former No. 10 jersey for a World Cup qualifying match — homage to a familiar low center of gravity, ball control, acceleration, change of direction, instinctive passing and flair for gasping brilliance. It was Messi's pass to midfielder Andres Iniesta that put

Barcelona into the Champions League final on an impossibly late goal against Chelsea.

"The most important game of my life," Messi said of Wednesday's match.

Three years ago, Messi was recovering from a thigh injury and did not bother to celebrate as Barcelona won the 2006 Champions League final over Arsenal in Paris. Last year, in the tournament's semifinals, he was quieted by Manchester United's left back, Patrice Evra. In fact, he has never scored against an opponent from the English Premier League, with its rigorous, physical defenses.

Even so, Messi has delivered 37 goals in various competitions this season and has offered the opinion that Barcelona deserves to win because of its beautiful attacking style featuring himself, Samuel Eto'o and Thierry Henry, who was expected to be available Wednesday despite a twitchy knee ligament.

"The world can see that he's the boss," Xavi Hernandez, the Barcelona midfielder, said of Messi, adding, "You can't compare him with anyone else because they will end up getting burnt."

Nicknamed the Flea, Messi is only 5 feet 7 inches and needed treatments of growth hormone as a pre-teen, a costly therapy that Barcelona agreed to underwrite after scouting him in Argentina and inviting him to a tryout at its youth academy in 2000. According to FIFA, soccer's world governing body, Messi was so impressive as a 13-year-old that Barcelona hurriedly signed him to a contract on a paper napkin.

A former teacher of Messi's once said that the only thing he liked about school was the bell, so he could run out and play soccer. As he turned 18, Messi was the top scorer for Argentina when it won the 2005 FIFA world youth championship. A year later, he became the youngest Argentine to play in a World Cup; already Maradona had begun to see in Messi something of himself — the way Messi escaped tight spaces and kept the ball so close while he dribbled, as if it were a pet obeying a leash law.

“The ball remains on the upper part of his foot, like it is glued to it,” Maradona said of Messi before the 2006 World Cup. “He feels the ball, and that makes him different from the rest. He’s also got another gear, a sixth gear.”

Quiet and largely unforthcoming, Messi keeps his words as close as he keeps the ball. His one display of youthful ostentation, a mane of long, stringy hair, has been shorn into a businesslike trim. His counterpart, Ronaldo, who has 26 goals this season, prefers a more metrosexual look in keeping with a personality that can be operatic and preening. Asked by a Brazilian newspaper last November who were the top three players in the world, Ronaldo smiled and said, “I am the first, second and third.”

Ronaldo, 24, is much bigger than Messi at 6-foot-1, and he may be more resourceful. He mesmerizes and menaces defenders as he runs at them, stepping over the ball in a kind of soccer River Dance, feinting and darting. He is threatening on headers. He can lash the ball on free kicks. And he will face a wounded Barcelona defense, which will be missing Daniel Alves, Eric Abidal and Rafael Marquez because of either red-card suspension or injury.

Ronaldo is “a great forward” who dribbles with speed and swerving ease, Messi told reporters. “And he has a great medium-range shot. We’re conscious that we can’t give him time to think or get a shot in from distance.”

This season at Manchester United has been accompanied by a prolonged drama about whether Ronaldo will soon leave for Real Madrid. In proclaiming last week that he was staying, Ronaldo did it in typically flamboyant style, saying, “My heart is here,” and calling Ferguson “a second father.”

Gerard Piqué, the Barcelona central defender and a former teammate of Ronaldo’s at Manchester United, told The Guardian of London that while Ronaldo was “a little vain when it comes to fashion and looking at himself in the mirror, he’s great fun and a very likeable person.”

Piqué added: "Ronaldo has everything — dribbling, shooting, heading and goals. He is one of the best players in the world. Only Messi can challenge him for that."

Ferguson has suggested that Ronaldo's greatness lay not in gaudy display, but in his workmanlike refining of his skills in those unseen moments alone after practice, when the cameras and the crowds are absent.

"If the big talents rely only on their natural ability, they won't have that extra edge," Ferguson said. "They must do something extra on their own."

That is exactly what the soccer world is expecting from Ronaldo and Messi on Wednesday — to produce something extra and fantastic on their own.

"I don't care about that," Ronaldo said about being considered the world's best player. "What I want more is to win the Champions League and that's it."

Ronaldo May Look Like the Best, but There Is Someone Better

BY ROB HUGHES | SEPT. 13, 2011

LONDON — If science could craft the ideal soccer player, the outcome might well resemble Cristiano Ronaldo.

He has the film-star looks. He is tall — 1.86 meters, or about 6-foot-1 — strong in the upper body, slender and swift below the waist. He has skill to burn and the desire of a peacock to display it bravely, often under aggressive attempts to kick him off his game.

The fact that Ronaldo might not be the best soccer player on earth — and that a comparative lightweight, Leo Messi, consistently beats him to the world player awards — spurs the Portuguese to seek self-improvement.

But what is inside the superstar? What would you find if you could break down the components and analyze them under laboratory conditions? In Ronaldo's case, there is now a documentary trying to do exactly that.

"Castrol Edge Presents Ronaldo Tested to the Limit" is a commercial film. Nobody would get access to conduct such experiments on a player of his stature without the commercial imperative.

Even so, the made-for-television documentary has some compelling insights. Ronaldo breaking glass panels by kicking a ball at 130 kilometers, or 80 miles, per hour; Ronaldo shooting literally in the dark; Ronaldo with electrodes attached to all parts of his body and Ronaldo wearing an eye contraption said to measure the speed at which his brain reacts to movement, are all fascinating setups.

Of course, there is commerce as much as science behind this. Sean Rahaley, the product's global brand manager, claims that, "By testing Ronaldo to his absolute limit, just like we do with the product, the film showcases the core brand values of Castrol Edge —

ELISA ESTRADA/REAL MADRID VIA GETTY IMAGES

Cristiano Ronaldo of Real Madrid jumps for a high ball during the La Liga match between Real Madrid and Espanyol at Estadio Santiago Bernabeu on September 21, 2010 in Madrid.

strength and performance — in an entertaining way." Entertaining, it certainly is.

The British university researchers and sports biomechanics analysts who spent weeks devising tests for the documentary had one full day with the star in Madrid. They worked him more than his coach, José Mourinho, might.

Stripped down, it was easy to show that he has the long legs of a sprinter, the leanness of a distance runner, yet the enhanced upper torso of a light-heavyweight boxer.

High-speed cameras confirm what we see of him in performance when his feet move at speeds that even the most practiced of defenders find bewildering. In one eight-second burst, he is filmed performing 13 moves, step-overs and spins.

He wears an eye-tracking device that uses infrared technology to detect what he is actually looking at during this test. "He did not look at the ball," said sports researcher Zoe Wimshurst, now of the University of Chichester in England and herself a junior international player in field hockey. "He as looking at the feet of the opponents and subconsciously assessing opportunities and moves." The tools available to the scientists can measure human reaction time down to 200 milliseconds. So when a proficient amateur player is asked to volley or head a ball driven toward him — with the light switched off at the instant the player providing the cross strikes the ball — he misses it by a good yard.

Ronaldo makes contact and scores a goal with each of three attempts at the same experiment. "It's almost as if he is doing the maths in his head," Wimshurst explained. "Although he probably couldn't describe it." This much, Ronaldo agrees. He knows that his reaction time is part gift, and part the result of countless times practicing, practicing, practicing.

His anatomy and his mind-set are gifts from his parents, though neither of them was an athlete. His love of the ball, and pronounced love of what he can do with it, are products of a childhood obsession that appears to have been self-generated even before Sporting Lisbon scouted him and took him from his Madeira Island home when he was 12.

Already obviously gifted, already willing to accept expert instruction, and crucially left alone to develop his individuality, the boy had entered the university of pro soccer.

The scientists, and the rest of us, are trying to play catch-up.

We are amazed, but not surprised, that he can strike a still ball at 20 meters with a force that shatters glass plates and with a speed measured at 130 kilometers per hour. The so-called Ronaldo knuckleball, where he hits a free kick with the flat of his foot rather than caressing it with his instep, still confounds even the researchers because he manages to impart swerve and spin, laterally as well as vertically, on the ball, as it deceives goalkeepers through the air.

And at that point in the fascinating hourlong documentary, a viewer might think: Thank God for the mystery. Thank goodness this is still a sport and not a science.

Thankfully, indeed, it is also a team sport in which players' performances are subjective. Ronaldo is mighty close to a record of scoring a goal for every one of the 93 games he has played for his latest club, Real Madrid.

However, he is not, as Castrol's commentary would have us believe, the ultimate player. Messi exceeds him because Messi creates as many goals for others as he scores for himself.

And there is a flaw in the Castrol ratings, just as there will always be flaws in applying science too intrusively to art. The rankings proudly proclaim to assess the best players in the game — but data is compiled only from the top five European leagues.

That means Neymar, the young Brazilian, is not included. It means his compatriot Leandro Damião, who has scored 39 goals over the past 12 months for Internacional in Brazil, and who is hot at the moment with 14 goals in 13 games, is anonymous, according to the ranking.

As to crafting, or even cloning, a perfect player. Castrol cannot do that, but Ronaldo has given it his best attempt. He has a son, Cristiano

SAMUEL ARANDA FOR THE NEW YORK TIMES

The island of Madeira, where Cristiano Ronaldo was born and where he also nurtured a childhood obsession with soccer.

Jr., born just over a year ago to a surrogate mother, and now being raised by Ronaldo's mother and sisters in Portugal.

Messi Named FIFA's Top Player for Fourth Year in a Row

BY ANDREW DAS | JAN. 7, 2013

LIONEL MESSI was honored as FIFA's world player of the year Monday for a record fourth year in a row. Messi, the 25-year-old Barcelona and Argentina star, received more than 41 percent of the vote, beating his rival Cristiano Ronaldo of Real Madrid, who was second at 23.6 percent, and two of his Barcelona teammates, midfielders Andres Iniesta and Xavi.

"To tell the truth, this is really unbelievable to get the fourth award," Messi said. "I am so nervous."

The vote was a signal of how dominant Spanish soccer, and especially its two cornerstone clubs, have become in the world game. The top six finishers all play in Spain, including three from Barcelona (Messi, Iniesta and Xavi) and two from Real Madrid (Ronaldo and goalkeeper Iker Casillas). Only the Colombian Radamel Falcao, a star striker for Atletico Madrid, broke their stranglehold; he finished fifth, just above Casillas, in voting by national team captains, coaches and selected news media members.

Ronaldo was the most serious challenger to Messi's victory, having scored a club record 46 goals to help Real Madrid end Barcelona's three-year run as Spanish champion. Messi scored 91 goals in all competitions last year, breaking Gerd Muller's 40-year-old world record for a calendar year, but he did not complete the feat until several weeks after voting had closed on Nov. 15. For that reason, perhaps, he seemed surprised to hear his name called again.

"My mind went blank and I couldn't think of what to say," he said.

Until Messi's recent run, Zinedine Zidane of France and Ronaldo of Brazil had been the only three-time winners of the FIFA award. The trophy was merged in 2010 with the Ballon D'Or, or Golden Ball, which had been awarded for decades by France Football magazine to the top player in Europe. That trophy was won three times by the French star Michel Platini and the Dutch forwards Johan Cruyff and Marco van Basten.

Forward Abby Wambach, who led the United States to the gold medal at the London Olympics, was voted FIFA's women's player of the year over another American, Alex Morgan, and Marta of Brazil. Vicente Del Bosque, who guided Spain to its second straight European Championship, and Pia Sundhage, who coached the American women to Olympic gold and then resigned after the Games, were honored as the coaches of the year.

In European Soccer, World Cup Is One of Many Priorities

BY ROB HUGHES | OCT. 22, 2013

LONDON — The moment that Portugal and Sweden were paired in a winner-take-all elimination process, media attention concentrated on the fact that either Cristiano Ronaldo or Zlatan Ibrahimovic would not be going to next year's World Cup finals.

The absence of one or the other will affect the tournament. Their presence unquestionably lifts any team they play for. While Sweden arguably has the greater team spirit to cope should anything happen to Ibrahimovic, the Portuguese have time and again been transcended by the singular skills, bordering on genius, of their captain, Ronaldo.

But the playoff games are not until Nov. 15 and Nov. 19.

This is soccer. This is a sport, a business, that leaves little time for buildup or preparation.

Maybe on Monday, when the playoff draw was made in Zurich, Ronaldo and Ibrahimovic, and their countrymen, thought about the World Cup. But by Tuesday, they had more urgent priorities.

Ronaldo is the highest paid player in the most expensive club side ever put together. He is part of the Real Madrid collection of players who meet Juventus in the Champions League — and the same collective travels to Barcelona for Saturday's "Clásico," the pivotal contest in the Spanish league season.

Is there is any other walk of life in which the principal protagonists are expected to be at peak performance in three such diverse tournaments in such a short time?

The schedule affords them no time to think. They play, they rest and recuperate, and if they are not injured they have to be ready to play again, in different circumstances, on different grounds, and perhaps with different teammates on their side.

Right now, perhaps, Ibrahimovic has the easier schedule. His Qatari pay-masters at Paris Saint-Germain have thrown enormous funds at lifting the French club and expect at least a run into the latter stages of the Champions League.

But Real has spent more, and will keep on spending more until the biggest prize in soccer — the European Cup — is back in its trophy cabinet.

"Real's philosophy remains the same," the veteran goalkeeper of Juventus, Gianluigi Buffon, commented in the Madrid sports paper Marca on Monday. "Buy great champions, entertain the fans, and maintain the historic prestige of Real Madrid."

He was referring to Madrid's so-called galáctico policy through which the current president, Florentino Pérez, has constantly spent world record sums to buy the players he deems to be the ones to bring "La Décima," the elusive 10th European Cup, to his Bernabéu Stadium.

Pérez, a construction magnate, is unashamed about his spending of Real's fortunes. As a boy, he watched with his father, Eduardo, as the greats, Alfredo di Stéfano, Ferenc Puskas et al., outplayed any opponents on earth. That team set the ball rolling on the first nine Cups, but not since 2002, not since the team built around Zinedine Zidane, has Real conquered the continent.

It is an obsession on which this president has spent all that the club earns, and more through bank loans. Real Madrid, Pérez says, is historically bound to be the best in the world. He once told me in the board room at the Bernabéu: "Whatever it takes, we will be again the institution that the whole world looks up to. Our history requires it."

Sports give you nothing for your history. You must buy it, build it, earn it afresh with every passing year, every tournament.

The reality today is that buying great players is not enough," Juve's Buffon said in Marca. "It is better to have a project, balance and patience. Money is a starting point, but it's not enough in itself."

Buffon spoke of Juventus as a team of quick tempo, highly organized, pressuring the opponents all over the field. Then he paused. Now 35, Buffon has won everything, including the World Cup, except the Champions League.

"But all the organization," said Juve's key man, "can go out of the window the moment Cristiano Ronaldo gets the ball, beats three players, and scores."

To Madrid's president, that must sound almost like an endorsement of the galáctico philosophy. Buffon mentioned only Ronaldo, but Real Madrid has paid more, in transfer fee terms, this summer to get Gareth Bale.

It has others — Ángel Di María, Karim Benzema and the exciting young Spaniard Isco — as attacking options. And if all those talents have yet to take La Liga by storm, the squad has shown its priority — its Real Madrid priority — this season by accumulating 10 goals in 2 Champions League games against Galatasaray and Copenhagen.

They will not find scoring such an easy touch against Juventus on Wednesday, despite the Italian champion's sudden loss of concentration in last Sunday's 4-2 Serie A defeat against Fiorentina.

But win, lose or draw against Juve, the Madrid players must regroup for the Clásico in Barcelona. This is a contest that stands apart from anything in Spain. It is fueled by politics, by Barça representing Catalonia against rule from Madrid.

In simple terms, it pits Ronaldo (again) against Lionel Messi. It matters beyond the outcome of the league title and beyond the fact that neither side, not Madrid nor Barcelona, has hit its stride in domestic soccer so far this season.

That might sound ridiculous, given that Barça is clear at the top of the league, with eight straight wins and a draw. But Messi has not yet been Messi this season. He has a court case over unpaid taxes hanging over him, he has been battling thigh injury and traveling to lead his country, Argentina, safely through World Cup qualification in the tough South American section.

Still brilliant. But so far this season, this has not been the Mesmeric Messi who year after year has outscored Ronaldo and inspired Barcelona to win the Champions League, and to capture world player of the year awards.

Messi will, barring injury, be at the World Cup next year. Ronaldo has hurdles to overcome, a nation to lift, before he can get there.

Relentless is our expectation.

Ronaldo Dethrones Messi as World Player of Year

BY SAM BORDEN | JAN. 13, 2014

IT DID NOT MATTER that the voting went mostly as expected; Cristiano Ronaldo cried anyway.

Ronaldo, the star forward for Portugal and Real Madrid, broke down in tears on Monday night after being named FIFA's world player of the year. He beat the Barcelona maestro Lionel Messi, who won the award the previous four years, and Franck Ribéry, the indomitable French midfielder for Bayern Munich.

Ronaldo, who scored 66 goals in 56 games last year, did not win a team trophy (Ribéry won five with Munich), but he did lead his national team to a place in the World Cup with a memorable performance against Sweden in the European playoffs. That star turn, in which Ronaldo scored all four of Portugal's goals in the two-leg matchup, came — coincidentally — just as FIFA extended the voting period for the year-end award, citing an unusually low response rate in the balloting.

That extension surely helped, though considering Ronaldo's productive scoring, as well as Messi's injury-plagued season and Ribéry's lack of gaudy statistics, his victory in the voting of national team coaches and captains and select journalists was largely expected. Ronaldo received 1,365 points, Messi 1,205 and Ribéry 1,127.

In truth, the player closest to Ronaldo in sheer quality, at least recently, was not on the final ballot: Liverpool's Luis Suárez, who has scored 22 goals in 16 English Premier League games this season. Suárez received only two first-place votes, but each came from a teammate. In other voting oddities, neither Messi nor Ronaldo listed the other in his top three, and Jurgen Klinsmann, the United States coach, left off both: Klinsmann voted for Ribéry, Gareth Bale of Wales and the Colombian striker Radamel Falcao.

Nonetheless, Ronaldo was ecstatic after his name was called at the end of FIFA's annual gala in Zurich. He dabbed at his eyes and was embraced by the Brazilian legend Pelé after the announcement. Ronaldo brought his young son, also named Cristiano, to the stage with him.

"I am very happy; it is very difficult to win this award," he said. "It is a tremendously emotional moment."

While Ronaldo's victory was not especially dramatic, the naming of the World XI — a global all-star team of sorts that is based on votes from as many as 50,000 professional players around the world — was emblematic of a growing parity among the top international teams.

In the past, the World XI had been dominated by Spanish and Brazilian players, with last year's edition being almost comically Iberian: all 11 players played in Spain, and 10 of the 11 played for either Real Madrid or Barcelona.

This year, however, for the first time since the World XI's inception in 2005, Germany was represented among the all-stars. The inclusion of Philipp Lahm, Manuel Neuer and Ribéry was fitting; after all, many observers saw last year's Champions League final between Bayern Munich and Borussia Dortmund as a symbol of the fast-rising stature of German soccer heading into this summer's World Cup.

Lahm, Neuer and Ribéry were not the only Munich representatives honored; Jupp Heynckes, who retired after Munich's sterling season, was also named the coach of the year.

"Maybe 10 years ago I wouldn't even have dreamt of this," said Heynckes, who saw Munich drop only 2 points in the second half of the season and clinch the Bundesliga title in April. "I am humbled and happy to be standing here."

Perhaps the biggest stunner of the evening came during the announcement of the women's player of the year. Abby Wambach, the

United States national team's productive forward and the winner of the award in 2012, figured to be favored along with Brazil's Marta. But Germany goalkeeper Nadine Angerer won for the first time.

"I have to say that I'm a little surprised," Angerer said.

CHAPTER 5

Controversies and Challenges

Throughout his career, Cristiano Ronaldo's professional and personal lives have been sources of controversy. He has been suspended for shoving referees, received yellow cards and the scorn of fellow players and fans for simulating falls, and been called out as a narcissist both on the field and in front of the press. He was also publicly scrutinized when he was charged with tax fraud in 2017 and accused of defrauding Spain of $16.5 million in taxes. These articles consider the various controversies surrounding Ronaldo and explore whether or not they are deserved.

Cristiano Ronaldo Banned Five Games for Shoving Referee

BY ANDREW DAS | AUG. 14, 2017

THE REAL MADRID star Cristiano Ronaldo was suspended for five matches on Monday by the Spanish soccer federation for shoving a referee who ejected him from a Spanish Super Cup match against Barcelona on Sunday.

The ban means Ronaldo will miss a second match against Barcelona on Wednesday, as well as the first four games of the Spanish league season that opens this weekend, unless it is overturned or reduced on appeal.

The incident that led to Monday's punishment occurred in the 82nd minute of Sunday first-leg Super Cup match at Barcelona's Camp Nou stadium. Ronaldo, running alongside Barcelona defender Samuel Umtiti at the edge of the penalty area, fell into the box after the players collided and appealed to the referee, Ricardo de Burgos Bengoetxea, for a penalty.

But De Burgos Bengoetxea deemed the tumble a dive, and awarded Ronaldo a yellow card for simulation. Since it was Ronaldo's second yellow of the match, De Burgos Bengoetxea then pulled a red card from his pocket and sent off the forward.

As he turned to head upfield, Ronaldo approached De Burgos Bengoetxea from behind and gently shoved him with his right hand.

Ronaldo's ban means he will miss the second leg of the Super Cup, on Wednesday in Madrid, as well as the first four games of the Spanish league season, which for Madrid opens Saturday at Deportivo La Coruña.

Ronaldo also was fined 3,805 euros, about $4,500. He and Real Madrid, which was fined about $2,000, have 10 business days to appeal the sanctions. Real Madrid left little doubt about its opinion of the ejection; the match report for Sunday's game on the club's website describes Ronaldo in its first sentence as "unfairly sent off."

Ronaldo's ejection capped a memorable, but brief, performance for the Portuguese star. Still working into game shape after an extended summer vacation, he entered the match as a substitute in the 58th minute, replacing the French striker Karim Benzema, and scored on a curling shot in the 80th.

He received his first yellow card after that goal, for removing his shirt to celebrate the score, which gave Real Madrid a late lead. Two minutes later, he was off.

Real Madrid won the match by 3-1.

A Victory for Portugal, but a Disappointment for Ronaldo

BY JEFFREY MARCUS | JUNE 14, 2012

WHEN JOAO MOUTINHO and his teammates ran to the corner of the field to embrace Silvestre Valera after the substitute put Portugal ahead of Denmark, 3-2, in the closing minutes of their Group B match Wednesday at Euro 2012, Cristiano Ronaldo fell to the grass and lay on the ground in the middle of the penalty box, alone, several yards away from the celebration.

His head, buried in the turf in Lviv, Ukraine, appeared to be elsewhere all game. At that moment, he might have been thinking about how fecklessly he missed the pass from Alexandre Fabio Coentrao that Valera then blasted into the back of the net. Before Valera pounced emphatically, Ronaldo, unprepared to receive the cross and facing away from goal, lamely reached back with his left leg, missing the ball entirely.

Or was he still thinking about his squandered breakaway opportunity only eight minutes earlier; when he put it harmlessly wide. He couldn't possibly still be thinking about how in the 50th minute he came in alone on Denmark's Stephan Anderson put the ball directly at the keeper, making it easy for him to save.

Somewhere, Fernando Torres was smiling because he knows how not funny it is to squander one give-me after another.

Portugal's coach, Paulo Bento, backed his superstar after the game. "He is a player of enormous ability who wasn't efficient in a couple of situations he found himself in," Bento said of Ronaldo. "He has played two good games. There is not a single player among the 23 in the squad who feels any sense of frustration."

It was difficult to believe Bento after watching the cameras show Ronaldo's face — pursed lips, droopy cheeks, eyes, all but tearing, cast lamentably skyward — during the game.

You never see Lionel Messi do that. You rarely hear Ronaldo compare himself with the Argentina and Barcelona forward who is his only peer in talent. But the frustration clearly got Ronaldo after the game with Denmark where he was taunted with patronizing chants from the fans in Lviv: "Messi! Messi! Messi!"

"Do you know where Messi was this time last year?" Ronaldo asked reporters after the game. "Do you know?"

"He was getting knocked out of the Copa America in his own country. I think that's worse, don't you?"

Pepe backs Ronaldo over Messi.

"Cristiano Ronaldo is the best player in the world but even the best make mistakes, so we're here to support him," said Pepe, his teammate for club and country. "He's just one more player in the team, he can't carry Portugal on his back."

Right or wrong, that's exactly what Ronaldo is expected to do because that's what he did for Real Madrid last season, scoring 60 goals in all competitions.

"Cristiano is O.K., he is happy, we won the game, so there is nothing to worry about," Nani, the Portugal midfielder, told reporters after the match. "Cristiano does not play alone, he is very important to us, his work rate was very good in my opinion, because he helped in defence and attack."

Russia's most important player, Andrey Arshavin, faced similar criticism as Ronaldo after his diminished effort against Poland on Tuesday. Though he provided the expertly placed free kick that Alan Dzagoev head-flicked in for a the goal, Arshavin faded and Poland came back to earn a much-deserved draw. After the match in Warsaw, Arshavin posted on Twitter, "The games was very exhausting for us [sic]."

His coach, Dick Advocaat, backed his player. "I'm tired from time to time, too," he said, also noting that Arshavin was "our most dangerous player."

"He was the sharpest with the ball," Advocaat said. "I did think about taking him off, but then he'd do something positive."

And that sums up the Little Tzar's reputation for frustrating inconsistency.

"For every bit of mind-numbing brilliance Arshavin provided against the Poles," wrote the Bleacher Report columnist Matthew Snyder, "there were the inevitably infuriating instances of wasteful dribbling and indifferent defending that threatened to erase all the good he'd done."

This reminds some of Arshavin's career at Arsenal, which may never resume. After watching him Tuesday against Poland, Ricardo Bernard wrote on Grantland, "I was reminded of why I once fell for him and why we simply can never be."

Is it unfair to criticize Arshavin for not living up to certain expectations? It may be a bit harsh seeing how he helped engineer a commanding 4-1 victory over the Czech Republic in Russia's first game, and was pivotal in the best moments against Poland.

But Arshavin is philosophical about it, and he said the dichotomy that he represents is a part of the Russian psyche.

"To put it simply, what lies in the Russian character, and why someone might consider us a dark horse, is that we can lose against every team and we can win against every team," he told UEFA.com, adding: "It's in the character of the Russian people that when we gather strength in our fist and we don't have anywhere to retreat to, we can win against any team. But if we relax a bit and follow our feelings, we can lose to a very weak team."

That means that Greece, Russia's opponent in the final group game Saturday, could be highly problematic. But Russia could very well go through to the knockout round with Arshavin only playing really good and not transcendent so long as Dzagoev keeps firing.

The CSKA Moscow midfielder has three goals in two games, and that might already be enough to earn him a lucrative move to a bigger club in Europe when the transfer window opens and his contract is up. Dzagoev, who appears to be the tournament's top breakout star so far, plays with unbridled enthusiasm that is in stark contrast to the burden of responsibility that Arshavin and Ronaldo seem to carry. It must be liberating.

"The first thing you know about this kid, apart from his talent, is that he doesn't play football for fame or money but because it is his life," Igor Rodkin, a Russian youth coach was quoted by the Independent in Britain. "He lives to win, he lives to play."

Dzagoev will turn 22 on Sunday, as Russia might very well be preparing for the second round of the European Championship.

Dear Ronaldo: It Isn't All About You

BY ROB HUGHES | SEPT. 11, 2012

LONDON — An open letter to Cristiano Ronaldo:

More than a week has passed since you set your latest phenomenal landmark as a Real Madrid player, and in the process blanked the fans at Bernabéu stadium.

You scored twice against Granada. You reached 150 goals for the club in 149 games, a faster scoring rate than Raúl, than Di Stéfano, Santillana, Puskas or any of the giants who made Real legendary.

Fabulous.

When you failed to show joy after the first of those two goals, some of us mistook your mood for humility. We actually thought that, with the ball going through the legs of Granada goalkeeper Toni, your gesture was that of a sportsman not wishing to gloat at a fellow professional's misfortune. But then it happened again. It was clear as you pursed your lips and shrugged off the congratulations of colleagues that something deeper was troubling you.

It is, of course, a sportsman's prerogative not to dance around and kiss the badge, or cuddle teammates, when you do your job. But let's face it: This isn't the norm for a player who, for Sporting Lisbon, for Manchester United and now for Real, has never been shy of sharing the love. There is a feature-length documentary, produced by one of your million-dollar sponsors, Castrol, to show off your prowess. Clearly, you reveled in making that video, which demonstrates that you are blessed with the perfect body for soccer and the dedication to work those quite extraordinary skills of coordination and athleticism that make you literally one in a billion.

From the day you walked into the Bernabéu, with tens of thousands packing the stadium just to see you set foot on the turf, you have exuded the self-awareness of being special in your sport.

So what, Cristiano, went wrong?

Why, after refusing to celebrate goals with colleagues and supporters in the home that guarantees your fortune, did you mysteriously say that you are sad, and the club knows why.

You are perhaps too young to have known Greta Garbo, the Swedish film actress who in midcareer quit Hollywood and spent a life in relative solitude, telling the news media, "I want to be left alone."

That was the lady's choice. She had made her money, she didn't much care for the intrusiveness of fame, and plainly it did not trouble her if she never shared her talents again with her followers.

You, Ronaldo, are at a different time and in a different career than Garbo.

The audience is part of your sport. It can help you win tight matches, and it deserves to share your ability to be such a game-changer.

Maybe you saw, or maybe your existence is too self-centered to have seen, the reciprocal joy that the Olympians — and just as exciting the Paralympians — have just shared with the world.

It is incredible to see men and women, sometimes in their teens, achieving far more than most of us with far less than you have been blessed with, feats of human striving and unforgettable exuberance. On one leg, or none, in a wheelchair or on prosthetic limbs, they performed to their maximum. Blind, they played your game by sound and a sense of movement.

Most of them laughed and cried because performing sports is about giving it all you have, and letting the emotions flow.

Many of us have been to games when your talents were decisive — and not merely the athletic gifts but the desire to lift a game, lift a performance. There were times at Euro 2012 in Poland and Ukraine when you transcended the sum of what the other 21 players on the field could achieve.

We applauded that, and you drank in that applause. You have done it so many times, and if there is a prima donna side to your nature, well, we forgive you that for all the moments when your feet dance, your shot soars, your spirit takes over a performance.

But what will not do is to turn away from the paying fans in your home stadium.

A part of you is public property. We know that Spanish soccer has to suffer some of the economic drain that is troubling the whole world, and that these are perilous times when the clubs of La Liga are in debt to the tax authority to the tune of €750 million, about $960 million.

Real Madrid is, apparently, the one club that does not owe the government money. And that is, in part, because Madrid enjoys privileged TV income and indulgent banking overdrafts whenever it overspends.

What you get out of that is, to a degree, your own affair. You arrived in Spain at a time when the government allowed what is known as the "Beckham Law," allowing David Beckham and other imported stars to face an eased tax burden. But Beckham has come and gone, and he was never in any case as talented as you.

Your aides insist that whatever your reason for sulking, money is not the core issue. However, the local news media run stories of Real's president preparing a way to keep on paying you more than your €12 million annual salary, without the 52 percent tax that other top earners must pay to the government.

If you had said your sadness was for Spain's five million unemployed, that would be a great public-relations play.

If, as many surmised, the sadness involves other players getting the accolades, that is less endearing. First it was Lionel Messi picking up FIFA's Ballon D'Or year after year. Now it is Andrés Iniesta being honored as the player of 2012 by UEFA, and for good reason: Iniesta was arguably the outstanding player of the 2010 World Cup, certainly the best in the final match. And Iniesta got Spain going when it retained the Euro championship title this July.

He's the quiet one, sometimes in Messi's shadow. And, if you need to ask, he wins people's hearts as well as their votes not simply because of his skills, but the pleasure he gives and takes in being a team player.

As good as you are, it isn't all about one man.

'Ronaldo Is the Most Annoying'

BY JEFFREY MARCUS | DEC. 10, 2010

LAST SUMMER, I talked to dozens of players, coaches and referees for an article about the scourge of international soccer: simulation.

"Much of the flopping, flailing and falling in soccer is little more than diving to the turf in an effort to dupe the referee," I wrote from South Africa. "Some of the best players in the world crumple under imaginary contact to win a penalty, or writhe in seeming pain to run the clock down or give their teammates a breather."

It is no mystery who some of those players are; many have a well-earned reputation for diving. But none of the referees I talked to — and few of the players — would say on the record who was the most notorious. Players didn't want to call one of their own a cheat, and referees did not want to appear prejudiced. Now, one of Europe's top officials has gone public, but the news is hardly shocking.

Claus Bo Larsen, a top referee from Denmark, told the Danish tabloid Ekstra Bladet that Cristiano Ronaldo "is the most annoying."

"He is always out to get a cheap free kick," Larsen said of Ronaldo, the Portugal and Real Madrid forward. "Especially at home."

"We talk in the locker room before the game that he goes down easily," Larsen added.

Would anyone who has watched soccer since the lithe Ronaldo came on the scene be surprised? Would you dispute Larsen's assessment? Who do you think is the most annoying diver?

When a Soccer Star Falls, It May Be Great Acting

BY JEFFREY MARCUS | JUNE 20, 2010

JOHANNESBURG — The Ivory Coast forward cried out in apparent agony, covered his face with his hands and dropped to the turf with a thud in the waning minutes of his team's 3-1 loss to Brazil on Sunday at the World Cup.

The forward, Abdul Kader Keïta, was not hit with the ball or slapped across the face or punched, just bumped by the Brazilian star Kaká, who did little more than shrug, sticking his right elbow into Keïta's chest.

That was all it took for Keïta to fall to the turf as if he had been doused with pepper spray.

The referee punished Kaká with a yellow card, his second of the game, forcing his ejection and leaving his team a man down for the rest of the game.

Many who saw the replay wondered whether Keïta's fall was the tournament's latest example of what officials call simulation. Much of the flopping, flailing and falling in soccer is little more than diving to the turf in an effort to dupe the referee.

If successful, the diver could be awarded an unimpeded kick from the point of the infraction or, if it occurs in the penalty area in front of the goal, a penalty kick from 12 yards.

Fans are already seeing as much bad playacting as tricky dribbling during the World Cup in South Africa, despite efforts by FIFA, the sport's world governing body, to punish divers. Some of the best players in the world crumple under imaginary contact to win a penalty, or writhe in seeming pain to run the clock down or give their teammates a breather.

"I wish it wasn't part of the game," said Paul Tamberino, the director of referee development for U.S. Soccer. "Players will do whatever they can."

In his first game of the tournament, the German midfielder Mesut Özil tumbled as if gnomes hiding in the grass at Durban Stadium had tied his shoelaces together during his team's opening game against Australia last week. An innocuous challenge from a defender did not seem enough to send him to the ground. Indeed, no foul was called. Instead, for his ruse, Özil was punished with a yellow card.

Özil's tumble and Keita's pantomime did not affect the outcome of either game; Germany and Brazil easily won their matches. But with so few games, and with goals at a premium at this World Cup (1.97 goals per game through the first 29 games, well below the low-water mark of 2.21 in 1990), an erroneously awarded penalty or unjust suspension could prove decisive.

In the Round of 16 at the World Cup in Germany four years ago, Italy and Australia were tied, 0-0, in added time. Italy's Fabio Grosso rushed into the Australia penalty area and doubled over the lunging defender Lucas Neill. Italy was awarded a penalty kick, converted it for a 1-0 victory and went on to win the title. The penalty kick eliminated Australia.

"When he slid in, maybe I accentuated a little bit," Grosso told Football Plus magazine in the spring. "I felt the contact, so I went down."

According to FIFA's Laws of the Game, "attempts to deceive the referee by feigning injury or pretending to have been fouled" are punishable by a yellow card. But it can be difficult at full speed, with only the naked eye and no video replay to consult, for a referee to spot the difference between a foul and a phantom.

The referee Koman Coulibaly whistled a foul in favor of United States forward Jozy Altidore in the 85th minute of the Americans' 2-2 tie with Slovenia on Friday — awarding a free kick that led to a controversial disallowed goal — but replays showed that minimal contact occurred before Altidore crashed to the ground. Players know they are more likely to get away with it and tacitly condone the practice.

"Personally, I'm against any type of simulation; I don't think it should be part of the game," Alessandro Del Piero, a teammate of

Grosso's, said recently, before adding: "It went in Italy's favor and I was happy. If it went against us, I would be upset."

Del Piero and his countrymen were indeed upset in 2002 when Italy was knocked out of the World Cup in South Korea by the host team after Francesco Totti was ejected for a second yellow card after disingenuously trying to earn a free kick.

Referees say that it is difficult to penalize a player for simulation because it is akin to calling him dishonest.

"If you're going to give a caution for simulation and there is contact," Tamberino warned, "it has to be very obvious that he's trying to cheat."

Sometimes, simulation is so transparent that it more resembles vaudeville than world-class soccer.

In 2002, Rivaldo of Brazil was waiting to take a corner kick when Hakan Unsal of Turkey appeared to deliberately kick the ball at him when he was not looking. Rivaldo went down as if he had been shot, clutching his face, right in front of an assistant referee. Unsal was given a red card, signaling an ejection, but Rivaldo was embarrassed when video replay revealed his reaction to be an act. FIFA later fined him $7,350.

"Whether it be the big flop or the big groan, sometimes it's comical," Tamberino said. "You don't like to laugh, but sometimes, you give a smile."

Referees must be close to the play and have the right angle and clear vision to make the correct call. It requires good positioning and communication between the referee and his assistants, one on each sideline. Three years ago, FIFA started a referee assistance program to train officials to, among other things, spot dives. Before the World Cup, FIFA's technical study committee provided referees and assistant referees with scouting reports, including video, that highlighted teams with a reputation for simulation.

Being a good diver may help a player get an occasional call, but when he earns a reputation as a cheat, it can be difficult to erase.

Portugal's Cristiano Ronaldo, one of the fastest and most dangerous forwards, is often the target of deliberate fouls or the victim of overzealous defenders.

"Referees should protect the more skillful players when they are getting fouled by the opposition," he said Tuesday after Portugal's game with Ivory Coast. "Sometimes it is difficult for me when the referees give fouls because they think I dive."

But they think that for good reason. Ronaldo was notorious for feigning when he was a young player. He was lethal on direct kicks, and he relished the chance to show off his ability to strike the ball from long range. But now that he has developed into one of the game's most hardened players, who is often hacked mercilessly by slower, less-skilled defenders, he does not get many calls.

"They don't protect talented footballers anymore," said Carlos Queiroz, the coach of Portugal. "I'd like to see if the rules are the same for everybody."

Players and referees say they know which players go down too easily, but they are reluctant to identify them.

"I'm anticipating all forwards are capable of doing that," said the American defender Oguchi Onyewu, who at 6 feet 4 inches and 210 pounds is an easy mark for conniving forwards who exploit the perception that a bigger player fouls more often.

"I think referees are taking the proper measures now more so than in the past to eliminate that kind of exaggeration," Onyewu said. "Giving the players themselves a card and not the defender."

But defenders and forwards agree that diving will be hard to eradicate as long as players get away with it.

"You try to get the ref on your side and you hope that he can see through all of that," said Jonathan Spector, a defender for the United States. "There's only so much you can control in a game. The call was made. Just get on with it."

In Europe, Young, Gifted and Limping

BY ROB HUGHES | SEPT. 20, 2011

LONDON — Who is to blame if the world's most gifted players become the objects of dirty play that can crush a career with a single swipe of the cleat? When the UEFA Champions League teams gathered in Monaco last month, Europe's chief refereeing officer, Pierluigi Collina, spelled out the priorities for the new season.

"We do not want to see broken legs," he said. "We do not want doctors on the pitch. We have to convince players not to put the safety of an opponent at risk."

The message was clear, that players should respect opponents, and referees should use their full array of powers when they do not.

But in the first round of Champions League matches, Cristiano Ronaldo of Real Madrid was hacked in the ankle, a wound that fortunately proved nothing more serious than a gash requiring four stitches.

In Real's next match, against Levante on Sunday, Ronaldo's teammate Ángel Di María sparked a brawl with a dangerous two-footed lunge that could have broken the leg of an opponent.

That same afternoon, Ashley Cole, the left back for Chelsea and England, got away with a tackle so high and so late that it was fortunate that his victim, Manchester United's Javier Hernández, known as Chicharito, has the leaping capability of a flea, which allowed him to escape the worst of the impact.

The players, coaches and officials are all failing to observe the kind of protection sought by Collina, a former referee. And if these are examples of so-called superstars at play, what example is being set for those down the scale who use physical aggression to compensate for a lack of skills?

Real Madrid Coach José Mourinho did something decent this week, donating his FIFA world coach of the year trophy to be auctioned for a cancer charity in the name of the man who had given him his start in team management, Bobby Robson.

But one good deed does not disguise or excuse the malice that is the other side of Mourinho's game.

Last week, one of his players, Ronaldo, was the victim of foul play in Zagreb, Croatia. His ankle was spiked by a Dinamo opponent, Jerko Leko. It was a late, apparently deliberate act. Svein Oddvar Moen, an inexperienced Norwegian referee, correctly whistled a foul, but he gave no card for the offense.

Leko had earlier been yellow-carded for another deliberate foul. But on the Ronaldo tackle, he said after the match, "I never intended to hurt Cristiano Ronaldo." He did, however, confess that Dinamo's instructions had been "to play a little harder than usual." If Dinamo had allowed Madrid players space to play, Leko reasoned, their superior talent would have exposed his team.

So the foul play was intentional, even if, according to Leko, the harmful consequence was not.

Unlike Moen, 32, and working his first season in the Champions League, Javier Turienzo Álvarez and Philip Dowd are experienced arbiters in the top leagues of Spain and England.

Mourinho blamed Álvarez for the violence that got out of hand during Real's 1-0 loss at Levante.

Álvarez did not kick anybody, but Mourinho's player Di María did.

His lunge at the legs of an opponent, with the ball nowhere near, was rash and dangerous petulance. It sparked pushing and shoving, during which Di María faked being injured and his colleague Sami Khedira was sent off for pushing down a Levante player.

Once again, the perpetrator, Di María, escaped a red card.

Mourinho used the postgame news conference to distort what people had seen.

"I don't want to take anything away from Levante's merit," he said. "As always, here at their home, they let them do what they want and they do it very well.

"I have only to congratulate them for being clever because they know how to provoke, they know how to fake it, they know how to gain time, they know how not to give the ball. They know the dirty side of football."

Mourinho, barred from the sideline in the Champions League and under investigation for his fit of pique in the aftermath of defeats to Barcelona, plays it both ways. The charitable man who knows all about the dirty side of soccer.

Perhaps the most inadequately punished foul Sunday was Cole's tackle of Hernández.

Cole regards himself as the finest fullback in the Premier League. But he was given the runaround by United's Portuguese wing, Nani. His frustration boiled and, his coach André Villas-Boas claimed, was exacerbated by two calls that allowed United goals that could have been disallowed for offside.

The decisions were marginal and favored the home team. But Dowd's worst call was to show only a yellow card for Cole's horribly mistimed lunge, with both feet off the ground, at Hernández.

Tests on Monday showed that the bone beneath Hernández's right knee was not broken, but that the flesh was badly bruised. Hernández and Cole escaped the worst of that foul, Cole twice over because though it clearly occurred inside the penalty box, Dowd issued no penalty kick.

If referees err, that is only human. Less excusable is when millionaire players threaten the livelihood of their fellow professionals, and coaches condone it.

Collina, it seems, was whistling in the wind in August.

Ronaldo, Under Fire, Strikes Quickly Before Slipping Away

BY ANDREW KEH | JUNE 21, 2017

MOSCOW — There was a collective murmur of surprise on Wednesday night when Cristiano Ronaldo swept into the interview room at Spartak Stadium in Moscow. So many of these journalists had so many questions for Ronaldo, the Portuguese superstar, and now here he was, rather unexpectedly, sitting right in front of them.

But the moment was short-lived.

"We're not going to have questions," the moderator said.

The reporters chuckled and groaned.

"Obviously we are very happy," said Ronaldo, whose goal had given Portugal a 1-0 victory over Russia in their Confederations Cup match. "It's the first time that Portugal has won in Russia. I think the team played well."

Another platitude or two, and he was gone. The whole thing lasted less than two minutes. It would have been shorter, except the microphone wasn't working at first, so Ronaldo had to wait a couple of seconds before he began speaking.

So for another day it continued, Ronaldo effectively hiding in plain sight while the rest of the soccer world gossips, speculates and, simply put, freaks out about him.

To catch up: Just last week, a prosecutor in Spain accused Ronaldo of defrauding the Spanish government of more than $16 million in taxes. A day later, he declared that "my conscience is clear."

But by Friday, the story went, Ronaldo was so upset by the accusation that he had decided he could no longer remain with his Spanish club, Real Madrid. The choice, to quote a Portuguese newspaper quoting unnamed associates of the player, was "irreversible."

The rumor mill quickly began churning out breathless reports, with each new one linking Ronaldo to any number of big clubs. Then, on Wednesday morning, hours before Ronaldo was to lead Portugal against Russia, a new story emerged — maybe. To quote a Spanish paper quoting more unnamed associates — or perhaps the very same ones — Ronaldo had been "comforted" to learn that Florentino Pérez, the Real Madrid president, had spoken publicly in his support. Ronaldo, the report said, was now willing to stay.

On and on the charade may go. Will he go? Will he stay? Was the whole thing concocted to deflect attention from the tax fraud accusations? Ronaldo will not say.

This particular sort of theater has a natural home in Europe, where the hugeness of soccer, the rabidity of the sports media and the relatively small responsibility that professional athletes here — compared to their counterparts in the United States — traditionally feel to speak to journalists can combine to create an environment of overheated intrigue.

When Fernando Santos, the coach of Portugal, entered the interview room after Ronaldo's short address, a journalist asked earnestly whether the coach thought the player had some sort of duty to comment on the stories whirling around him, many of which seemed to be coming from his own camp.

"He's here to talk about the game, not about his family, about Real Madrid," Santos said. "I understand you're all curious. You have to understand — and I'm saying this with a good feeling — we have to respect the personal life of a player. It doesn't bring anything positive."

So Ronaldo went about his job on a cool, hazy afternoon in Moscow. The home fans whistled when he appeared on the video screen before the match and whistled again, even louder, when he first took possession of the ball just over two minutes into the match.

Eventually, Ronaldo made clear once again why people fuss over him. All those games, all that mileage on his legs, and he continues to supply a stream of big goals and indelible moments. He has counteracted the aging process by becoming more surgical in his play, more judicious with his running, more attuned to opportunities in the air.

Playing alongside the hard-working Andre Silva, Ronaldo was allowed to hover menacingly on the periphery of the action. In the eighth minute, he lurked along the edge of the penalty area as play bubbled far off on the left wing. When the ball was finally served into the goal mouth, Ronaldo drifted to the far post and placed his head to it, barely leaving his feet, depositing it into the goal just beneath the crossbar.

He jogged, scowling, to the right corner and celebrated with his teammates in the suddenly quiet stadium.

"We missed Ronaldo," said Stanislav Cherchesov, the coach of Russia, referring to the defense on the goal. "But that's just not us, judging by how many golden balls he's won."

These have been a fascinating — and productive — last few weeks for Ronaldo. In the Champions League final on June 3, he scored twice against Juventus to help Real Madrid defend its title, its third in four seasons. Ten days later, a state prosecutor accused him of defrauding the Spanish tax office of 14.7 million euros, about $16.5 million, in unpaid taxes from 2011 to 2014. He has been summoned to testify in court on July 31 in Madrid, two days after Real Madrid plays its archrival Barcelona in a summer friendly in Florida.

It may take until then to hear him personally comment on the case, or his future.

Late Wednesday night, after the goal and the celebrations and the curt performance in the news conference room, Ronaldo had to walk through one more room full of reporters to reach the team bus. With gold headphones slung around his neck and a team press official at his side, he marched toward the door as a few intrepid journalists gamely, but hopelessly, lobbed questions at him.

He stopped only once, to sign an autograph for a smiling reporter. The request technically represented a breach of protocol — journalists are forbidden to ask athletes for autographs — but at least someone got something out of him.

Outside, a Russian-accented chant of “Ro-nal-do!” emerged from a throng of waiting fans. The players wordlessly boarded the bus, which then peeled off into the blue Moscow night.

CHAPTER 6

Athlete or Celebrity?

More than just an athlete, Ronaldo is a celebrity. Ronaldo's personal life is often subject to scrutiny. His forays into fashion and displays of wealth cause some people to question whether he is more concerned with fame than athletic success. Others criticize Ronaldo for not using his influence to advocate for political and social issues, the way some celebrities do. However, this ignores the fact that Ronaldo has on multiple occasions made generous charitable contributions and come to the aid of young fans, helping to fight the poverty he encountered growing up.

Real Madrid Fans' Generational Divide

BY KABIR CHIBBER | NOV. 3, 2009

MADRID — When he wasn't mumbling Spanish obscenities to himself, the distinguished-looking older gentleman sitting next to me at the Santiago Bernabeu on Saturday cried out: "A Kaká! A Kaká!"

Other Real Madrid fans stood, flailing their arms in desperation, imploring the players to pass the ball to the Brazilian. A cheer went up when the team listened and Kaká received the ball to run forward against the Getafe defense.

But not everyone was as focused on Kaká as my neighbor. The teenagers and children and groups of young tattooed men chewing sunflower seeds (leaving them in piles on the floor) didn't seem to much care who had the ball. Their player, Cristiano Ronaldo, was out with an ankle injury.

NEW PRESS/GETTY IMAGES

Ricardo Kaká of Milan in action during the Serie A match between Parma and Milan at the Stadio Tardini on Febraury 16, 2008 in Parma, Italy.

There has been a gentle civil war for the affections of Madrid fans since the summer when Kaká joined from A.C. Milan for $92 million, the second largest transfer fee of all time, after world-record signing Ronaldo arrived in Spain for $131.5 million a few days later.

Many of the younger Madrid fans at the stadium Saturday for the Spanish league match against Getafe (Madrid won, 2-0) wore Ronaldo's No. 9 shirt and styled and gelled their hair like the Portuguese star, who will missed Tuesday's Champions League clash with A.C. Milan, a 1-1 draw.

But for all his talent, Ronaldo's brashness, his flashy clothes and celebrity romancing don't endear him to the older generation of fans with their graying moustaches, impeccably trimmed, sitting in the cheap seats and listening to radio commentary of the game on earpieces.

Kaká moves around the field as if he were royalty, which is the way the Madrid fans who remember some of the team's nine European titles think of the "King's Club," courtesy of King Alfonso XIII in 1920.

The Ronaldo crew grew up in the first "Galacticos" era of Figo, Ronaldo, Beckham and Zidane. They measure success not in terms of trophies won but money spent. They are envious of Manchester City, not disgusted.

Ronaldo has missed six games with an ankle injury, which has coincided with a poor run of form, including a humiliating 4-0 drubbing last week by third division Alcorcon in the Copa del Rey. Madrid have won all of the games that Ronaldo has played, and he's still the team's top scorer.

Kaká hasn't yet achieved the form that defined his time at Milan, scoring only three goals in all competitions this season.

Today, Kaká gets another chance to prove himself — in Ronaldo's absence — against his old club. When Madrid and Milan met two weeks ago, the Rossoneri won spectacular game, 3-2. Milan's striker Marco Borriello tried to needle Kaká, saying he was past his prime. The 27-year-old playmaker responded: "I am sure he was only joking."

After World Cup, It's Worlds Apart for Top Players

BY ROB HUGHES | JULY 18, 2010

THE WORLD CUP is history. One week after it ended, the players rated No.1, 2 and 3 in the world by FIFA have gone their separate ways.

Lionel Messi, who dazzled until his Argentina team lost in the quarterfinals, spent Thursday at a Unicef site visiting orphans and homeless children still suffering the aftermath of January's earthquake in Haiti.

Cristiano Ronaldo, who scored once before Portugal left the tournament in the first knockout round, announced on his Web site and his Facebook and Twitter pages that he had become the father of a son born during the first week of the tournament. The mother is an American woman he apparently paid to be a surrogate.

Wayne Rooney left the World Cup after barely displaying a trace of his skills before England was bounced by Germany. Rooney is now vacationing in Barbados, where he and his wife, Coleen, released a statement over the weekend saying how relieved they were after winning a court case brought by his former management company, which claimed it was owed millions of pounds.

So while the Uruguay forward Diego Forlán stole the show as the outstanding player of the World Cup, it becomes apparent that the big three had other things on their mind.

Ronaldo's pride in fatherhood, and his method of publicizing the fact, is pretty much his own affair, though the timing might explain his somewhat distracted performances in South Africa.

Rooney's court verdict, held over until the World Cup was finished, was not offered as an excuse for his tired form in June and July. But it cannot have helped that every penny made by Rooney and his wife — they are England's second-biggest celebrity soccer couple — was being debated by lawyers in open court.

JOSEP LAGO/AFP/GETTY IMAGES

Frequent opponents — Barcelona's Argentine forward Lionel Messi (R) vies for the ball with Real Madrid's Portuguese forward Cristiano Ronaldo during the Spanish league 'clasico' football match FC Barcelona vs Real Madrid on November 29, 2010 at Camp Nou stadium in Barcelona.

Messi's first calls after the World Cup — a charity soccer game in Panama, followed by a trip to visit homeless refugees outside Port-au-Prince, Haiti — showed a different set of priorities.

On Wednesday, he scored a hat trick in leading his team, Leo Messi & Friends, to a 6-4 victory over the Rest of the World in an exhibition game to raise funds for impoverished Panamanians. The next day, he flew to Haiti, where he visited Carrefour Aviation, a camp housing 50,000 people in tents after the devastation of the January quake.

Since he agreed to become a Unicef ambassador in March, this was Messi's first exposure to the world beyond the five-star cocoon of playing for Barcelona and being one of the most prized athletes on earth. His humility as he hugged and kissed orphans in Haiti, his concern when he met and was briefed by U.N. peacekeepers from Argentina, were evident.

"I have never seen anything like this," he said. "There are few places in the world where children are facing such dangers." And then, amid high security, he was gone.

His club, Barcelona, pays to carry the Unicef logo on its team jerseys. But you can imagine Barcelona's relief, too, when its greatest player came through both the charity match in Panama and the visit to Haiti without a scratch.

Manchester United, meanwhile, has begun its North American preseason warm-ups without Rooney.

The club is reported to be renegotiating a contract that pays him £120,000, or $185,000, a week. It would increase that amount by about 25 percent — another £30,000 a week — to keep predators like Real Madrid and Chelsea at bay.

Rooney's performance with his club last season was the opposite of the way he played with England. The goals he scored for Manchester United had kept the team competitive in the English and European leagues. His tireless running, often through injury, had sustained his club.

Quite possibly, he had nothing left to give at the World Cup. Arguably, Manchester United is a more gifted squad than England. Reports from inside England's camp in South Africa suggested that the discipline imposed by England's coach, Fabio Capello, was too much for the players to take.

Whatever the reasons, whatever the excuses, not one England player lived up to his billing. But if Rooney was counting the days to his Caribbean holiday with his wife and baby son, the court was counting, and surprisingly making public, every last dime the Rooneys have earned since his emergence as a 17-year-old prospect.

In those days, Rooney received an apprentice wage of £80 per week. As his fame grew, as he — a young bull among men — showed skills and tenacity beyond his peers, the marketing men began throwing riches at his feet. And eventually at the feet of Coleen, his sweetheart who became his wife.

His earnings from soccer, and from global brands like Nike and Coca-Cola, and her salaries from celebrity columns and TV shows, were detailed in Manchester Mercantile Court, where an agency claimed the Rooneys owed them £4.5 million in commission for deals brokered on their behalf.

The problem was that Paul Stretford, a founding partner of the agency Proactive, had quit the firm and taken Rooney with him. The judge's verdict on Thursday was that Proactive's contract represented restraint of trade because it covered eight years, while the English Football Association recommends a maximum deal of two years between player and agents.

Judge Brendan Hegarty awarded the agency just £90,000.

Rooney then issued a statement. "Fortunately the judge knocked back their massively overinflated claims," it read. "We are happy to pay the very small sum awarded.

"I was shocked that a company which represents some of Britain's biggest entertainers was going down this road, which meant that private financial and commercial matters were made public," the statement read. "They first claimed that Coleen and I owed them £8.3 million, then £4.5 million. These sums were a joke and we felt they were just an attempt to exploit us."

The couple, who are in their early twenties, had earnings valued at £35 million. As the lawyers and agents battled to rake in a percentage of those earnings, it is worth pondering what that money could do in Haiti or Panama, where it could make a real difference.

How Superstars' Pay Stifles Everyone Else

BY EDUARDO PORTER | DEC. 25, 2010

This article was adapted from "The Price of Everything: Solving the Mystery of Why We Pay What We Do," by Eduardo Porter, an editorial writer for The New York Times. The book, to be published on Jan. 4 by Portfolio, examines how pricing affects all of our choices.

IN 1990, the Kansas City Royals had the heftiest payroll in Major League Baseball: almost $24 million. A typical player for the New York Yankees, which had some of the most expensive players in the game at the time, earned less than $450,000.

Last season, the Yankees spent $206 million on players, more than five times the payroll of the Royals 20 years ago, even after accounting for inflation. The Yankees' median salary was $5.5 million, seven times the 1990 figure, inflation-adjusted.

What is most striking is how the Yankees have outstripped the rest of the league. Two decades ago. the Royals' payroll was about three times as big as that of the Chicago White Sox, the cheapest major-league team at the time. Last season, the Yankees spent about six times as much as the Pittsburgh Pirates, who had the most inexpensive roster.

Baseball aficionados might conclude that all of this points to some pernicious new trend in the market for top players. But this is not specific to baseball, or even to sport. Consider the market for pop music. In 1982, the top 1 percent of pop stars, in terms of pay, raked in 26 percent of concert ticket revenue. In 2003, that top percentage of stars — names like Justin Timberlake, Christina Aguilera or 50 Cent — was taking 56 percent of the concert pie.

The phenomenon is not even specific to the United States. Pelé, from Brazil, the greatest soccer player of all time, made his World Cup debut in Sweden in 1958, when he was only 17. He became an instant star, coveted by every team on the planet. By 1960, his team, Santos, reportedly paid him $150,000 a year — about $1.1 million in today's money. But these days, that would amount to middling pay. The top-paid player of the 2009-10 season, the Portuguese forward Cristiano Ronaldo, made $17 million playing for the Spanish team Real Madrid.

Of course, the inflated rewards of performers at the very top have to do with specific changes in the underlying economics of entertainment. People have more disposable income to spend on entertainment. Corporate sponsorships, virtually non-existent in the age of Pelé, account today for a large share of performers' income. In 2009, the highest-earning soccer player was the English midfielder David Beckham, who made $33 million from endorsements on top of a $7 million salary from the Los Angeles Galaxy and AC Milan.

But broader forces are also at play. Nearly 30 years ago, Sherwin Rosen, an economist from the University of Chicago, proposed an elegant theory to explain the general pattern. In an article entitled "The Economics of Superstars," he argued that technological changes would allow the best performers in a given field to serve a bigger market and thus reap a greater share of its revenue. But this would also reduce the spoils available to the less gifted in the business.

The reasoning fits smoothly into the income dynamics of the music industry, which has been shaken by many technological disruptions since the 1980s. First, MTV put music on television. Then Napster took it to the Internet. Apple allowed fans to buy single songs and take them with them. Each of these breakthroughs allowed the very top acts to reach a larger fan base, and thus command a larger audience and a bigger share of concert revenue.

Superstar effects apply, too, to European soccer, which is beamed around the world on cable and satellite TV. In 2009, the top 20 soccer teams reaped revenue of 3.9 billion euros, more than 25 percent of the combined revenue of all the teams in European leagues.

Pelé was not held back by the quality of his game, but by his relatively small revenue base. He might be the greatest of all time, but few people could pay to experience his greatness. In 1958, there were about 350,000 television sets in Brazil. The first television satellite, Telstar I, wasn't launched until July 1962, too late for his World Cup debut.

By contrast, the 2010 FIFA World Cup in South Africa, in which Ronaldo played for Portugal, was broadcast in more than 200 countries, to an aggregate audience of over 25 billion. Some 700 million people watched the final alone. Ronaldo is not better then Pelé. He makes more money because his talent is broadcast to more people.

If one loosens slightly the role played by technological progress, Dr. Rosen's framework also does a pretty good job explaining the evolution of executive pay. In 1977, an elite chief executive working at one of America's top 100 companies earned about 50 times the wage of its average worker. Three decades later, the nation's best-paid C.E.O.'s made about 1,100 times the pay of a worker on the production line.

This has separated the megarich from the merely very rich. A study of pay in the 1970s found that executives in the top 10 percent made about twice as much as those in the middle of the pack. By the early 2000s, the top suits made more than four times the pay of the executives in the middle.

Top C.E.O.'s are not pop stars. But the pay for the most sought-after executives has risen for similar reasons. As corporations have increased in size, management decisions at the top have become that much more important, measured in terms of profits or losses. Top American companies have much higher sales and profits than they did 20 years ago. Banks and funds have more assets.

With so much more at stake, it has become that much more important for companies to put at the helm the "best" executive or banker or fund manager they can find. This has set off furious competition for top managerial talent, pushing the prices of top-rated managers way above the pay of those in the tier just below them. Two economists at New York University, Xavier Gabaix and Augustin Landier, published a study in 2006 estimating that the sixfold rise in the pay of chief executives in the United States over the last quarter century or so was attributable entirely to the sixfold rise in the market size of large American companies.

And therein lies a big problem for American capitalism.

Capitalism relies on inequality. Like differences in other prices, pay disparities steer resources — in this case, people — to where they would be most productively employed.

Despite the great danger and cost of crossing the border illegally into the United States, hundreds of thousands of the hardest-working Mexicans are drawn by the relative prosperity they can achieve north of the border — where the average income of a Mexican-American household is more than $33,000, almost five times that of a family in Mexico.

In poor economies, fast economic growth increases inequality as some workers profit from new opportunities and others do not. The share of national income accruing to the top 1 percent of the Chinese population more than doubled from 1986 to 2003. Inequality spurs economic growth by providing incentives for people to accumulate human capital and become more productive. It pulls the best and brightest into the most lucrative lines of work, where the most profitable companies hire them.

Yet the increasingly outsize rewards accruing to the nation's elite clutch of superstars threaten to gum up this incentive mechanism. If only a very lucky few can aspire to a big reward, most workers are likely to conclude that it is not worth the effort to try. The odds aren't on their side.

Inequality has been found to turn people off. A recent experiment conducted with workers at the University of California found that those who earned less than the typical wage for their pay unit and occupation became measurably less satisfied with their jobs, and more likely to look for another one if they found out the pay of their peers. Other experiments have found that winner-take-all games tend to elicit much less player effort — and more cheating — than those in which rewards are distributed more smoothly according to performance.

Ultimately, the question is this: How much inequality is necessary? It is true that the nation grew quite fast as inequality soared over the last three decades. Since 1980, the country's gross domestic product per person has increased about 69 percent, even as the share of income accruing to the richest 1 percent of the population jumped to 36 percent from 22 percent. But the economy grew even faster — 83 percent per capita — from 1951 to 1980, when inequality declined when measured as the share of national income going to the very top of the population.

One study concluded that each percentage-point increase in the share of national income channeled to the top 10 percent of Americans since 1960 led to an increase of 0.12 percentage points in the annual rate of economic growth — hardly an enormous boost. The cost for this tonic seems to be a drastic decline in Americans' economic mobility. Since 1980, the weekly wage of the average worker on the factory floor has increased little more than 3 percent, after inflation.

The United States is the rich country with the most skewed income distribution. According to the Organization for Economic Cooperation and Development, the average earnings of the richest 10 percent of Americans are 16 times those for the 10 percent at the bottom of the pile. That compares with a multiple of 8 in Britain and 5 in Sweden.

Not coincidentally, Americans are less economically mobile than people in other developed countries. There is a 42 percent chance that the son of an American man in the bottom fifth of the income distribution will be stuck in the same economic slot. The equivalent odds for a British man are 30 percent, and 25 percent for a Swede.

NONE of this even begins to account for the damage caused by the superstar dynamics that shape the pay of American bankers.

Remember the '80s? Gordon Gekko first sashayed across the silver screen. Ivan Boesky was jailed for insider trading. Michael Milken peddled junk bonds. In 1987, financial firms amassed a little less than a fifth of the profits of all American corporations. Wall Street bonuses totaled $2.6 billion — about $15,600 for each man and woman working there.

Yet by current standards, this era of legendary greed appears like a moment of uncommon restraint. In 2007, as the financial bubble built upon the American housing market reached its peak, financial companies accounted for a full third of the profits of the nation's private sector. Wall Street bonuses hit a record $32.9 billion, or $177,000 a worker.

Just as technology gave pop stars a bigger fan base that could buy their CDs, download their singles and snap up their concert tickets, the combination of information technology and deregulation gave bankers an unprecedented opportunity to reap huge rewards. Investors piled into the top-rated funds that generated the highest returns. Rewards flowed in abundance to the most "productive" financiers, those that took the bigger risks and generated the biggest profits.

Finance wasn't always so richly paid. Financiers had a great time in the early decades of the 20th century: from 1909 to the mid-1930s, they typically made about 50 percent to 60 percent more than workers in other industries. But the stock market collapse of 1929 and the Great Depression changed all that. In 1934, corporate profits in the financial sector shrank to $236 million, one-eighth what they were five years earlier. Wages followed. From 1950 through about 1980, bankers and insurers made only 10 percent more than workers outside of finance, on average.

This ebb and flow of compensation mimics the waxing and waning of restrictions governing finance. A century ago, there were virtually no regulations to restrain banks' creativity and speculative urges. They could invest where they wanted, deploy depositors' money as they saw fit. But after the Great Depression, President Franklin D. Roosevelt set up a plethora of restrictions to avoid a repeat of the financial bubble that burst in 1929.

Interstate banking had been limited since 1927. In 1933, the Glass-Steagall Act forbade commercial banks and investment banks from getting into each other's business — separating deposit taking and lending from playing the markets. Interest-rate ceilings were also imposed that year. The move to regulate bankers continued in 1959 under President Dwight D. Eisenhower, who forbade mixing banks with insurance companies.

Barred from applying the full extent of their wits toward maximizing their incomes, many of the nation's best and brightest who had flocked to make money in banking left for other industries.

Then, in the 1980s, the Reagan administration unleashed a surge of deregulation. By 1999, the Glass-Steagall Act lay repealed. Banks could commingle with insurance companies at will. Ceilings on interest rates vanished. Banks could open branches anywhere. Unsurprisingly, the most highly educated returned to banking and finance. By 2005, the share of workers in the finance industry with a college education exceeded that of other industries by nearly 20 percentage points. By 2006, pay in the financial sector was again 70 percent higher than wages elsewhere in the private sector. A third of the 2009 Princeton graduates who got jobs after graduation went into finance; 6.3 percent took jobs in government.

Then the financial industry blew up, taking out a good chunk of the world economy.

Finance will not be tamed by tweaking the way bankers are paid. But bankers' pay could be structured to discourage wanton risk taking. Similarly, superstar effects are not the sole cause of the stagnant incomes of regular Joes. But the piling of rewards on our superstars is encouraging a race to the top that, if left unabated, could leave very little to strive for in its wake.

3 Modern Soccer Gods and One Bad Apple

BY ROB HUGHES | OCT. 24, 2010

LONDON — Over the weekend, Pelé, the greatest player of them all, celebrated his 70th birthday — and three young pretenders of the modern era strutted their stuff.

Lionel Messi scored both goals in Barcelona's 2-0 victory at Zaragoza on Saturday. Andrés Iniesta, his teammate, was given a standing ovation from beaten fans on their home ground, a show of gratitude that all of Spain feels toward the modest hero whose goal won the World Cup last summer.

Later Saturday night, Cristiano Ronaldo scored four goals in 36 minutes during Real Madrid's 6-1 rout of Racing Santander.

Not one of them will score a thousand times in a thousand games for one club, as Pelé did for his beloved Santos. Not one will win three World Cups, as Pelé did with Brazil between 1958 and 1970.

But Messi, Iniesta and Ronaldo should always be rich in money and in memories. These are the modern gods of the game. Pelé is old school. What has not changed is that proof of player power is done in the stadiums. All the rest — the fame, the transient glory and what we nowadays call image rights — is secondary.

It is good, very good indeed, to see what Messi, Iniesta and Ronaldo did this weekend. It is a pleasurable contrast to the supposed player power exhibited by Wayne Rooney and his manipulative agent when they held Manchester United to ransom last week.

Rooney is not a fit player at the moment. His ankle is injured, and while his team played on Sunday, he was having the biggest 25th birthday bash money could buy at his country mansion.

His celebrations may have included managing to extort double his salary from United despite the worst six months of form in his time at the club. He did that by threatening to leave unless Manchester's

U.S. owners put the already indebted club deeper into debt by signing players whom Rooney considers worthy of sharing the field with him.

Some called Rooney's stand a Eureka moment. Some simply think it reeks.

Contrast it with Messi, who, on hearing that Inter Milan's owner, Massimo Moratti, is contemplating a world record bid to lure him from Barcelona, responded politely: Thanks for the compliment, Mr. President, but I'm Barça's for as long as I'm wanted.

Contrast it with Iniesta, a flyweight in physical size, a mighty man in achievement and a one-club team man since the day he joined Barcelona's academy at the age of 12. Iniesta will play in any position, anytime, for his team.

Even contrast it with Ronaldo, a former colleague of Rooney's at Manchester United. For sure, Ronaldo was the real star of the team while he was there. Yes, he chose to leave when Real Madrid called his number. And certainly he can be a preening, prancing, prima donna.

But United's manager, Alex Ferguson, let him go, and would welcome him back anytime. The manager realized that the player, born on the Portuguese island of Madeira, quite genuinely had a childhood dream of playing in Real Madrid white, a calling to perform in what he sees as the greatest arena in his culture.

It was, I think, significant that the good answers to the bad vibes of the Rooney saga came in Spain. La Liga is different from the English Premier League in one essential detail: It is less of a physical contest, more a test of skill on the ball.

The Spanish league is dominated by its two monolith clubs, Barcelona and Real Madrid, for reasons that embrace politics, tradition and the clubs' ability to write their own global TV contracts. England is more equitable in that the television gold is shared among the 20 teams, but it is no different in the way money determines where the top players play.

United is a match for Madrid in world marketing. Were Pelé to play today, it is more than likely he would have played for one of the Spanish giants. He had offers, but he stayed faithful to Santos until, at his career's end, he played out a two-year sinecure with the New York Cosmos.

Pelé made a million or two, but the Rooneys and Ronaldos of this world make that in a few months.

Star players today are like the stars of Hollywood once upon a time. They know their worth in the entertainment package, and they barter for it.

Where Rooney steps outside the business surrounding the sport is the way he, or his greed-ridden agent, Paul Stretford, showed utter disrespect to the team, the club, the norms of negotiation.

Rooney's performance since last March, exacerbated by his not-so-private life, made him a liability, not an asset, to his team. Yet he had the gall to make his demands public last Wednesday, while his mates on the team did all the running.

It's a quirk of player power.

How much more acceptable was the power of Messi, in game after game, to apply himself to the team, to score where others may not and to applaud his teammates for making their chances.

How much better that Ronaldo, feeding off the empathy that is rising week by week at Real Madrid, should score goals by the hatful, and then say it is a great feeling, but a shared feeling.

"Some of my teammates were better than me tonight," he said Saturday. "But like the coach says, there is no reason to be euphoric. There is a long way to go in the league, although being top is important."

The coaches of Real Madrid and Barcelona know their teams are privileged, the opposition sometimes pitiable. They know that the head-to-head matches between the big two, the first of which is a month away, might determine who is best.

And Madrid kept its euphoria grounded this weekend in a particular way. The club had invited four of the 33 miners rescued from the collapsed mine in Chile to be special guests in the Bernabeu stadium. The players and the miners, workers world apart, mutually celebrating a game.

Poparazzi: The Manly Business of Gossip

BY BEN WIDDICOMBE | JULY 13, 2010

TRADITIONALLY MEN HAVE THOUGHT of gossip as something cavewomen invented to pass the time while the guys were out hunting mastodons. It was considered a frivolous, and definitely unmanly, pastime.

But what was true for 40,000 years seems to have changed dramatically in the space of half a generation. Celebrity stories that once would have simmered in a gossip column, like Lindsay Lohan's recent sentencing to 90 days in jail, now saturate the culture and dominate the news cycle.

I believe the reason for this cultural shift is that gossip (or "celebrity news," if we're feeling formal) is now an acceptable subject for men. And the emergence of sporting figures as international celebrities has made it easier for men to be interested in subjects like marriages and relationships that were once, as the Brits might say, strictly for the birds.

Tiger Woods's infidelity scandal was the biggest soft news story of 2009, riveting both men and women. That was quickly followed by another celebrity divorce, this one involving Sandra Bullock and her unfaithful husband, Jesse James, whose ultra-masculine image as the C.E.O. of the motorcycle customizer West Coast Choppers was a hook for male curiosity.

It's only a short step from that to following Cristiano Ronaldo, the 25-year-old Portuguese soccer sensation. Days after his team was ejected from the World Cup in South Africa, he turned up to meet his girlfriend in New York on the same weekend he announced that he had just fathered a baby with an unnamed woman. It was not only his female fans who found that interesting.

TMZ, the Los Angeles gossip franchise that produces a Web site and a weekday television show, offers an interesting study in tone. Its subject matter is largely interchangeable with other gossip sites like Perez Hilton's, who writes with a high-camp style that plays up his flamboyance and Miami-Cuban heritage. Reading Hilton's Web site sometimes feels like being best friends with Charo.

TMZ, however, gives it to you "straight." Its voice, reinforced by a daily TV show shot in the bullpen, sounds more like a conversation you'd have in a locker room, albeit one in which the main topic is celebrity sex tapes. This is a significant development for a field that had been dominated in magazines by women writing for women and online by gay men.

Crucially, TMZ (and similar sites like RadarOnline.com) manage to appeal to men without turning off the female audience. TMZ eschews traditional areas of women's interest — "babies and relationships" — but revels in the misdeeds of NFL stars and flashy real estate transactions of NBA players. The formula has been so successful that TMZ's founder, Harvey Levin, has announced plans to spin off TMZ Sports into its own site.

Gossip about athletes touches themes of money and sex that are also present in the usual stories about Hollywood stars, but until recently it seemed inappropriate for a man to care about another man's marriage. After Tiger Woods, that is no longer the case — and even the non-gossip media have picked up on the trend. Recent ESPN coverage of the Woods divorce settlement has delighted in treating the numbers like sports stats, gleefully comparing the reported dollar amounts with those of other athletes. It didn't seem to matter that the subject was the players' personal lives and not their performance on the field.

In an era when the mastodons come frozen from the supermarket, it seems that men have discovered there might be something interesting about this "gossip" thing after all.

Nice Goal! How'd You Like to Be a Model?

BY ERIC WILSON | JULY 7, 2010

DURING A TYPICALLY unremarkable performance at this year's World Cup, in which the United States team was ousted in the Round of 16, there was at least one crowning achievement for the Americans, a shot heard around the world.

As it happened, that shot was taken by a camera, when the team's hunky captain, Carlos Bocanegra, was photographed with Bill Clinton, celebrating the American victory over Algeria on June 23. The resulting image — Mr. Bocanegra grinning with his shirt off, he and the former president drinking Buds — was posted on the Twitter account of a Sports Illustrated writer and reposted to so many blogs that the young soccer star caught an unexpected glimpse of fame in his home country, a nation that more typically reserves celebrity worship for local weather forecasters than for soccer stars.

Could Mr. Bocanegra be the next David Beckham or Cristiano Ronaldo?

He seems to be cultivating a real-man-who-likes-fashion image in a way that few of his predecessors have, without drawing a metrosexual penalty. For example, Mr. Bocanegra, who bears an elaborate tattoo of his own surname on his left shoulder, told Interview magazine that his favorite historical period is Roman times: "Just real rugged and manly men. You know, ripping meat apart with their teeth." Yet, in the same article, he said he likes Gucci loafers and white Nixon watches.

It should come as little surprise that fashion designers have had their antennae up for a breakthrough star at the World Cup. After Messrs. Ronaldo and Beckham modeled for Mr. Armani, and Louis Vuitton produced a campaign that pitted Pelé against Zinedine Zidane and, during the men's shows last month, half of Milan was plastered with Dolce & Gabbana underwear ads featuring Italian players, who's left? A new batch of potential underwear models and fragrance pitchmen needs to be discovered.

"If you, as a fashion brand, want to connect with mainstream guys in Europe, it is vitally important to make that association with soccer," said Nick Sullivan, the fashion director of Esquire. "It's like the 'bat phone' way of reaching guys who are not necessarily going to go and buy Vogue. Putting soccer players in their underwear is like saying to these guys, 'This is cool.' "

That said, Mr. Sullivan has found this year's Most Fashionable Player draft picks to be underwhelming. He is keeping an eye on Thiago Silva, a 25-year-old Brazilian who plays for the Milan league and therefore includes some of the world's most prominent designers among his fan base

"It's not a vintage year," he said. "The ones they really need have to be dazzlingly good-looking, be good with their feet and be willing to be a fashion plate."

Alas, some of the best players in the world you would not wish to see on a billboard in their briefs. Lionel Messi of Argentina, an international player of the year, "is not such a good-looking lad," said the men's-wear designer Simon Spurr, who is English and therefore objective because his team doesn't do well enough to advance at the World Cup. Wayne Rooney, the powerful English forward, has the looks of a bulldog — and, evidently, a tattoo, after a Stereophonics album, that says "Just Enough Education to Perform."

Mr. Spurr's money is on Fernando Torres, the sometimes-blond striker for Spain with boy-band looks who already has his own watch collection and an autobiography. On the other hand, Mr. Torres, 26, is called El Niño and might appear just a little too wholesome.

"It's rare when you get a Ronaldo or Beckham," Mr. Spurr said. "It's hard to find that all-in-one package these days. When they come about, the fashion brands jump on them."

Some of the other players who are beginning to blip on the fashion radar include Japan's Keisuke Honda, whose notices for his ash-blond hair have rivaled those for his dead-aimed goals; and Iker Casillas, a goalie who looks like a Spanish Josh Hartnett and was dubbed by People (of all people) as "the next big thing."

"Iker definitely has the potential to be turned into a 'brand,' much like Ronaldo or Beckham," said Christian Cota, a designer who was born in Mexico City but follows the Spanish team as well. Carlos Miele, a Brazilian designer, ranked Messrs. Bocanegra and Torres highly, and cited Roque Santa Cruz of Paraguay, Alexandros Tzorvas of Greece and Yoann Gourcuff of France as promising.

Although these names may be virtually unheard of in the United States, you may nevertheless find yourself buying underwear from them soon.

"I met Beckham when he was 18 and he was already a guest at Donatella Versace's house," Mr. Sullivan said. "He was already being courted then. And that was before Victoria got her hooks into him and sorted out his hair."

In 2017, Many Athletes Found Their Voices

BY CHRISTOPHER CLAREY | DEC. 20, 2017

IT WAS THE YEAR when athletes got political again, very political.

By the time December arrived, it seemed more routine than incendiary when Lindsey Vonn, the star American skier, made it plain in a CNN interview that she would not be accepting an invitation to the White House if it were extended after the coming Winter Olympics.

She said she would be representing her nation at the Games but not President Trump. "I am proud to be an American, and I want our country to continue to be a symbol of hope, compassion, inclusion and world unity," Vonn said later, in another sign of the times, on her Instagram account. "My travels around the world have recently made clear that this is no longer how people view the United States. You cannot pick up a newspaper or turn on the TV in Europe without noticing how people are questioning our direction."

In a different era, Vonn, with her extensive list of corporate sponsors and hard-earned prominence in a niche sport, might have been the sort of well-entrenched figure who would have determined that she had much more to lose than to gain by taking a stand (or a knee) on a polarizing matter.

There are still ample risks: see Colin Kaepernick's current employment status after leading the way on national anthem protests in the N.F.L., or the menacing messages Vonn said she received from Trump supporters.

But there is no doubt that Vonn was part of a sports chorus in 2017.

"I think 'take a knee' has really taken on a life of its own and spearheaded everything else that's been going on," said the former tennis champion Martina Navratilova, 61, who came out as a lesbian and often spoke up — to her own commercial detriment — during her remarkable career. "Things always kind of operate by waxing and waning. This has been a big spurt, and it's not done yet, because it hasn't really been resolved one way or the other as far as I can tell."

The chorus has been amplified by the megaphones of social media and also by the old-fashioned snowball effect in a time of societal shifts and global tension, not all of it generated by the American president.

When one superstar goes public with strong personal views, it makes it less risky for the next. There is also the mentor factor. When a leading coach, like Steve Kerr of the Golden State Warriors or Gregg Popovich of the San Antonio Spurs, is so outspoken — and eloquent — on political issues, it is less risky for players to follow their lead.

"Maybe during the Michael Jordan era, there was the idea that sponsors would frown upon this sort of thing, but the consequences I think are a lot more complex," said Roger Pielke Jr., a political scientist and the director of the Sports Governance Center at the University of Colorado Boulder. "As athletes cross the lines that were maybe once taboo and they learn that the consequences are either not negative or, if you're LeBron James or Steph Curry, maybe even positive, I think we'll see more of it because that's the incentive structure."

Could "Just Say It" become the new mantra to sell shoes?

That depends on whether this surge in athlete activism is truly a new paradigm or whether it is part of the same cycle that led from Muhammad Ali and other Vietnam-era sports stars to the apolitical, resolutely mercantile approach of Jordan and Tiger Woods in a less fraught time.

"I think now because of the situation we have in our country, reporters are more apt to ask political questions of athletes," Navratilova said. "Kaepernick kind of opened that door again. We thought we were past it, but we're not. When Obama was elected, I was like, O.K., we don't need to worry about racism nearly as much anymore.

And now it's worse. We're going backwards, which is why I think the athletes are speaking out more, because we are going backwards on so many fronts."

What is evident is that the internet's capacity to make the distant seem personal is not going away. Whether they are asked political questions or not, athletes, like other celebrities, will continue to be able to deliver their messages — be they solipsistic or deeply civic — directly and immediately to the public, no gatekeepers required.

The paradox is that Kaepernick, the former San Francisco 49ers quarterback, is more symbol than spokesman (he has declined many offers from universities and others to speak). His decision to sit and later kneel during the national anthem before games in 2016 in protest over racial inequality and police violence was the spark that led to the flame and other anthem protests from prominent athletes, including the American women's soccer star Megan Rapinoe.

But the flame turned into a genuine bonfire only in September when Trump politicized the issue by criticizing the patriotism of N.F.L. players and urging owners to take action.

It was the N.F.L. that mandated players be on the field for the anthem, beginning in 2009.

"By the N.F.L. using athletes as props to try to market America as part of the N.F.L., they also gave athletes power to protest," Pielke said.

The protests angered Trump, and led to tweets that involved the president and two of the biggest American stars: Curry and James.

When Trump withdrew a White House invitation to Curry — the point guard who had led the Golden State Warriors to the N.B.A. title but who did not plan on making the usual celebratory appearance at the White House — James weighed in on Twitter.

"U bum @StephenCurry30 already said he ain't going! So therefore ain't no invite. Going to White House was a great honor until you showed up."

Athletes not only used their celebrity and new communication tools to get political in 2017. J.J. Watt, the star defensive lineman for the Houston Texans, started a fund-raising campaign to help Houston after Hurricane Harvey and raised more than $37 million.

Others, like members of the United States women's national soccer and hockey teams, reaped the financial rewards after taking strong public stands about their right to better pay and working conditions.

But while athlete activism was most audible in the United States in 2017, sports figures spoke out elsewhere, too.

Prominent Australian athletes — including Australian Rules football players and rugby league players — urged their compatriots to vote yes in the same-sex marriage postal survey that eventually led to Australia legalizing same-sex marriage in December.

In Spain, athletes were weighing in or being asked to weigh in on Catalonia's independence referendum, despite the Spanish government deeming it unconstitutional.

Rafael Nadal, back at No. 1 in the tennis rankings, did not hesitate to respond when asked. "I can't imagine Spain without Catalonia, and Catalonia without Spain; I don't want to see it," said Nadal, who is from Majorca and grew up speaking Catalan and Spanish.

But more than 20 other Catalan athletes and coaches openly declared their support for independence. Pep Guardiola, the Manchester City coach and former Barcelona star and coach, spoke at a pro-independence rally earlier in the year.

Though the Spanish government would declare the referendum illegal and take measures to block it, Gerard Piqué, the star Barcelona defender, was adamant that the Catalans should have had the right to vote.

In the wake of the violence sparked by the government crackdown, Barcelona played a home game at the cavernous Camp Nou stadium against Las Palmas behind closed doors without spectators. Piqué was later booed and whistled as he took part in a Spanish national team training session.

Though Piqué declined to say how he would have voted, he offered to leave the Spanish national team if Coach Julian Lopetegui believed it was best (Piqué stayed).

"Politics is a drag, but why shouldn't I express myself?" Piqué told reporters. "I understand those players who don't want to say anything. We're footballers but we're people too. Why can a journalist or a mechanic express themselves but not a footballer?"

But unlike the biggest stars and leading coaches in the N.B.A., the planet's leading men's soccer players have been much more reluctant to get political or even topical. They are restricted by club and national team policies and pressures, by concerns about sponsor reaction but also by their own proclivities.

In 2015, Cristiano Ronaldo abruptly and profanely ended a CNN en Español television interview, which he had agreed to with the aim of promoting a new line of headphones, when he was asked about the FIFA corruption scandal and the 2022 World Cup in Qatar.

"I don't care about FIFA, and Qatar!" he said.

But there is no doubt the impact would be powerful if the Ronaldos, Messis and Neymars of the world were to find their voices on societal, political and soccer governance issues.

The questions and opportunities will keep coming. There are plenty of flash points ahead, including next year's World Cup in Russia, where human rights remain a major issue, just as they did when the Russians hosted the Sochi Winter Olympics in 2014.

Beyond that are the European Games in Minsk in authoritarian Belarus in 2019, the 2022 Winter Olympics in Beijing and the 2022 World Cup in Qatar.

"If you look at the calendar in the short term to 2018 and then beyond to 2022, you have some of the biggest human rights abusers hosting the biggest sports events," said Minky Worden, director of global initiatives at Human Rights Watch. "With Russia at least, you have a perfect storm of all the major human rights abuses. They had North Korean slave labor building the St. Petersburg stadium.

They've got laws restricting freedom of protest and expression. They've been arresting journalists as recently as last week and crushing civil society and of course there's still the anti-gay law on the books with the added terrifying exhibit of the recent anti-gay purge in Chechnya."

Will athletes speak out in 2018 in a way they did not or felt they could not in Sochi? Or will they decline to take the risk, which Navratilova makes clear is still there.

"I was lucky because I played an individual sport and couldn't be kept out," she said. "If I'd been playing on a college basketball team and I come out, the coach doesn't put me in, and I don't get to play. With Kaepernick, if he were a golfer or tennis player, he would still be playing, so rotten luck."

Ronaldo . . . for the Defense

BY JACK BELL | OCT. 14, 2013

HEADING INTO THE FINAL DAY of the group stage of World Cup qualifying in Europe, Portugal requires a mini-miracle to overtake first-place Russia in Group F and avoid a two-game playoff with an opponent to be determined.

After yielding a late goal to visiting Israel and settling for one point on Friday, Portugal trails Russia by 3 points before its match against lowly Luxembourg. Russia plays at Azerbaijan needing only a point to win the group.

And while Portugal and Cristiano Ronaldo prepared for the final two qualifiers last week, the Real Madrid star took time out to send a letter to officials in Florida in defense of the man who jumped out of the stands at Sun Life Stadium in Miami Gardens, Fla., last summer and embraced Ronaldo in perhaps the sweetest, most benign on-field encounter between a fan and a player in sporting history. (Note that Ronaldo received a yellow card in the match against Israel and is suspended for Tuesday's game. While he will miss the low-risk match against Luxembourg, the yellow card on Friday ensures that he has a clean disciplinary slate for a potential playoff.)

The encounter with the fan came during the final of the Guinness International Champions Cup against Chelesa over the summer. The fan, was Ronald Gjoka, a 20-year-old college student and resident of Canada who was born in Albania. Gjoka had jumped the advertising boards and rushed to Ronaldo; the two embraced and shared an intimate chat on the field. While most professional athletes are loath to encourage interlopers when they invade fields of play, Ronaldo stood calmly and listened to Gjoka before he was escorted off the field by security personnel. The young man spent nearly three days in jail after the incident before he was charged.

Gjoka apologized to tournament and stadium officials, and to Ronaldo, but he still faces trespassing charges in Florida after failing to get the charges dismissed early last week.

The Spanish sports daily Marca published the text of the letter written by Ronaldo to the judge and prosecutor in Florida pleading for leniency for Gjoka:

> *My name is Cristiano Ronaldo and I play for Real Madrid. I was playing in Sun Life Stadium when a fan entered the field.*
>
> *His name is Ronald Gjoka, a young college student. We hugged, and we spoke for a while, until security arrived to escort him off the field. He was not aggressive or violent in ANY way. What's more, he did not put up any resistance when the security guards and police arrived.*
>
> *As I understand it, he has admitted his mistake and understands the importance of security. He is a young man of twenty who grew up without a father and was raised by a single mother. He attends Palm Beach State Community College, Florida, with an international student grant.*
>
> *I am concerned because I understand he may face problems with immigration and with his college if the criminal charges against him are not dropped. He was immediately taken to the Stadium's security area and then spent a day and a half in jail.*
>
> *It seems he appeared before a judge on Monday accompanied by his attorney who asked for the charges to be dropped, but you chose to ignore his appeal.*
>
> *I understand your position and the importance of enforcing rules and laws. However, I respectfully request that you and your office reconsider this decision and dismiss the two criminal charges this young man faces.*
>
> *I would hate to see him face criminal charges for his mistake. By all accounts he has a bright future ahead of him and I'd hate to see this future ruined by an error of judgement. Thank you. If you have any questions please don't hesitate to contact me directly at any time.*
>
> *Sincerely,*
> *Cristiano Ronaldo*

European Stars to Play for Charity

BY JACK BELL | JAN. 12, 2009

SOME OF THE BIGGEST STARS of European soccer have agreed to participate in a charity match in June at Giants Stadium in East Rutherford, N.J., for the benefit of Mikael Silvestre's charity, Schools for Hope.

Silvestre, a French international defender who plays for Arsenal of the English Premier League, started the charity with the goal of building educational institutions around the world. So far, Schools for Hope has built schools in Niger and Guinea, and is seeking financing for additional schools in Laos, parts of South America and perhaps the United States.

"When my children first started to go to school, I realized that education is the basis for a better life for poor children everywhere in the world," Silvestre said in a telephone interview from London. "I said to myself that I want to act, I want to be involved, with my own money. The focus is not on football at these schools; it is getting a good education, basic skills and professional skills, so the students are able to go out and get a good job."

The match, on June 14 against an opponent to be determined, is being called All-Stars for Hope (allstarsforhope.org).

The European contingent, in addition to Silvestre, will include Thierry Henry (France/Barcelona), Didier Drogba (Ivory Coast/Chelsea), Wayne Rooney (England/Manchester United), Cristiano Ronaldo (Portugal/Manchester United), Nicolas Anelka (France/Chelsea), Emmanuel Adebayor (Togo/Arsenal), Manuel Almunia (Spain/Arsenal), Frank Lampard (England/Chelsea) and Ryan Giggs (Wales/Manchester United). Silvestre said he hoped to enlist Arsenal Manager Arsène Wenger as the all-stars' coach and perhaps to entice Pierluigi Collina out of retirement to work the game as the referee.

"We want to have the game in New York because I think that is the best way to get the players involved," said Silvestre, who has a strained thigh muscle that will keep him out of action for three weeks. "After a long season in Europe, they don't want to do the game in London or Paris, they would find three days in New York to be more attractive. They want to go away from where they live, and New York sounds more like a holiday place. It's magic when you say New York, and some of the players have never been."

Silvestre said that the school in Guinea would graduate its first class this year. The school in Niger's capital, Niamey, draws children whose parents are lepers or otherwise disabled. He said it took about $68,000 to operate the schools for two years. He said the hope was to raise funds to complete work at the school in Laos, and there are plans for schools in Brazil, Argentina, Burkina Faso and perhaps New Orleans.

All the money raised from the sale of tickets to the game, Silvestre said, will go to the charity. An auction of memorabilia and items signed by players and teams (like a jersey signed by all the members of Manchester United's Premier League and Champions League winners) will also benefit the charity.

"I want to make sure this is an entertaining game, a good show," Silvestre said. "We want the fans to come back, maybe in two years' time again in New York."

SPAIN

Jozy Altidore, the young American striker who plays for Villarreal, confirmed Monday that Everton of the English Premier League was interested in acquiring him.

"I'm not going to lie, I'm young and my first thought was playing time," Altidore said in a telephone interview. "It would have been a quick fix for six months, but maybe not the best thing in the long run. I understand that the people at Villarreal want me to succeed, and I want to repay their faith in me."

Altidore has appeared in five games for Villarreal in La Liga and scored one goal.

"Yes, there was definitely something at Everton," he said. "But Villarreal said they wanted me here, and I'm fine with that."

Ronaldo on Track to Eclipse Beckham's Riches

BY JEFFREY MARCUS | APRIL 22, 2010

CRISTIANO RONALDO continues to follow David Beckham. Both players wore No. 7 at Manchester United, where they had tremendously successful and lucrative spells for a club that is itself the epitome of soccer success. Ronaldo, like Beckham before him, moved from England to Spain, to play for Real Madrid. And now, the Portuguese wing appears poised to follow the former England captain to the top of the soccer economy.

According to Forbes, Beckham is the highest-paid soccer player in the world, earning $40 million in 2009, $33 million from endorsements with Adidas, Giorgio Armani and Motorola. He outpaced Ronaldo by $10 million, though this is almost certain not to last.

Beckham sustained a torn Achilles tendon and will not play in the World Cup in South Africa. His absence from the sport's premier international event is expected to hurt his sponsorship income. The L.A. Galaxy midfielder will turn 35 on May 2 and his international career is almost certainly finished. How long he will continue to play in Major League Soccer will depend on his recovery from injury. He has two years left on his contract.

Ronaldo, who moved from Manchester United to Real Madrid for $131.5 million last summer, has deals with Nike, Coca-Cola and, like Beckham, Giorgio Armani. The 25-year-old will play for Portugal in South Africa this summer and will continue to play for one of the world's biggest clubs for years to come.

His Real Madrid teammate, Kaka (another well-heeled member of team Giorgio Armani) is next on the Forbes list, earning $25 million, along with another Brazilian, Ronaldinho of A.C. Milan, who earns about the same. Two Barcelona players, Thierry Henry of France ($24 million) and Lionel Messi of Argentina ($20 million) come next.

Chelsea and England teammates Frank Lampard ($17 million) and John Terry ($16 million) are Nos. 7 and 8. Zlatan Ibrahimovic, the Sweden and Barcelona striker, also made $16 million, but he, like Beckham, will not play in the World Cup because Sweden failed to qualify. England's Steven Gerrard, the Liverpool midfielder, rounds out the top 10.

With Fame Comes Power for Global Sports Stars

BY ROB HUGHES | JULY 10, 2009

LONDON — The sporting superstar has reached a level of global recognition beyond any film star.

"There is no movie star in the world who could get thousands of people to wait six hours just to see their arrival, as Cristiano Ronaldo did this week," said David Puttnam, filmmaker turned law maker in the British House of Lords.

Puttnam, who over 30 years produced award-winning films, including "Chariots of Fire," "The Killing Fields," "Bugsy Malone," and "Memphis Belle," is certain that Tom Cruise could not hope to draw 80,000 to a movie theater the way Ronaldo did to his signing ceremony at Real Madrid's Bernabéu stadium last Monday.

"I have watched the dynamic of the superstar shift from film to sports," Puttnam added. "The whole level of globalization of sports is bigger. The key is engagement. The power of sport has taken the movie industry by surprise."

We were speaking at the Beyond Sport summit meeting in London where Puttnam — now Lord Puttnam, legislator and ambassador for Unicef — joined people from government offices to ground workers in some of the world's most violent crime spots to discuss the power of sports.

Fame need not be frivolous. Puttnam, 68, has witnessed the emergence of celebrity added to charitable causes, from Danny Kaye, the American actor, singer and dancer of the 1950s, to the David Beckham phenomenon today.

He shared a panel at Beyond Sport with Tony Blair, the former British prime minister now working on reconciliation between Israelis and Palestinians. Beside them was Prince Faisal Al Hussein, adviser to Jordan's armed forces as well as the founder of Generations for Peace, which attempts to use sport to unite youth.

And besides them was Dikembe Mutombo, a former N.B.A. star now using his stature back home in the Democratic Republic of Congo to construct hospitals and research centers in his hometown of Kinshasa. Mutombo went to the United States on a scholarship hoping to become a doctor. He returned to Africa as more than a doctor, using fame and fortune, to try to turn the tide of H.I.V.

He appeals to soccer in particular to put more back into a continent, which European clubs have plundered of so many star players.

Even down to Ronaldo, there is a social conscience that should not be overlooked. Showmanship is a major part of his talent, and playing the prima donna is second nature to him.

Yet this same performer who loves the crowd to love him also, at the relatively unknowing age of 20, was one of the first in to Aceh Province after the tsunami devastation of December 2004. Touched by the bravery of a boy found wandering the beach, lost after most of his family were washed away in the horror, Ronaldo paid for the boy to attend a match involving his own national team, Portugal.

The player, then at Manchester United, flew to Indonesia to give his time and presence to raise more than a billion rupiahs, then about $90,000, toward rebuilding homes.

"I never cease to be thrilled by some of the players I meet and the way they handle all that surrounds them," Puttnam said at Beyond Sport. "The Barcelona club pays Unicef to wear our logo on the shirts, and more than that I've talked to the players.

"They tell me they get a thrill representing the world's children. I've never had the same conversation with Manchester United players about A.I.G." The United shirt is sponsored by the American insurance company, though the club has worked for nine years with Unicef without going that extra step that Barcelona did in paying the charity to wear the insignia.

But nobody supposes that sports clubs are anything less than big businesses these days. The fusion of cricket and Bollywood captures the modern world — and the worlds of celebrity, sport and entertainment.

Blair, the politician discovering the extraordinary pulling power of sports, said: "Most world leaders I have met enjoy something about sport, and some even play. But I think over the years it has become of a different magnitude, and we are only just beginning to understand the utility of sports." He recalls going into a classroom in Japan and trying to relate to children. "I was introduced as the prime minister of Britain," he says. No response. "I tried to say London." A flicker.

"Then I said Beck-ham ... Ah, yes, I had a response." Blair said that the more he learned about the power of government, the more he also discovered the limits of government. Sport, he suggested, could sometimes unlock those limitations.

Later, sitting besides Michael Johnson, the American sprinting icon, Blair admitted: "You know, Michael, when I told my own family who I was meeting today, they were suddenly interested. My kids are used to me talking about world leaders, but a real live sporting superstar, that was something different." As we left the room, Blair took the opportunity to have his photograph taken with Johnson. For the children, no doubt.

It was reminiscent of Carlos Menem, the Argentine president from 1989-99, appointing Diego Maradona as a sporting ambassador for the world. The president shamelessly courted the soccer star, basked in his popularity. He didn't know that at that time, leading up to the 1990 World Cup in Italy, Maradona had already begun the drug addiction in Naples that ultimately destroyed him as a player, and almost as a man.

This is heady stuff, when politicians and the rest of us put the fleeting stars of sports high on a pedestal, asking some of them to sort out the world's problems.

Glossary

aficionado A person who is very knowledgeable and enthusiastic about a particular subject.

ample Plentiful or enough.

audacious Willing to take bold risks.

benign Gentle, not harmful in effect.

cornerstone An important feature or component upon which something is based.

curling shot A kick in which the ball spins in a way that causes it to change direction.

defraud To illegally obtain money through deceptive means.

detriment Harm or damage.

emphatically In a forceful way.

entrenched Firmly established and difficult to change.

federation An organization or group that is broken down into smaller divisions.

feint A pretended movement meant to deceive an opponent.

flamboyant Attracting attention because of exuberance or stylishness.

forward A player who plays nearest to the opposing team's goal in soccer.

frivolous Lacking serious purpose or value.

intrinsic Essential and naturally belonging to something.

leniency Being more merciful than anticipated.

manifest To make clear or obvious.

mawkish Oversentimental.

nullify To cancel out or make of no use.

ostentatious Meant to impress or attract attention through a pretentious display.

pernicious Having a gradually harmful effect.

petulant Bad tempered, sulky, or childish.

polarize To cause to divide by sharply contrasting groups or sets of beliefs.

prerogative A privilege exclusive to a particular individual.

prima donna A temperamental person with an inflated sense of self worth.

proclivity One's inclination or preference for a particular thing.

prowess Skill or expertise in a particular field.

query A question.

resilience The ability to recover quickly from difficulties.

roster A list of the members of a team or organization.

saturate To supply something to the point where the demand for the product is more than satisfied.

saunter To walk in a relaxed manner.

singular Exceptional or remarkable.

slog Working hard over a long period of time.

sortie Attack or assault.

squander To recklessly waste something.

supplant To replace or override.

thespian An actor.

transient Impermanent, lasting for a short time.

unabated Without any reduction in intensity.

winger An attacking player who plays toward the side of the field in soccer.

Media Literacy Terms

"Media literacy" refers to the ability to access, understand, critically assess, and create media. The following terms are important components of media literacy, and they will help you critically engage with the articles in this title.

angle The aspect of a news story that a journalist focuses on and develops.

attribution The method by which a source is identified or by which facts and information are assigned to the person who provided them.

balance Principle of journalism that both perspectives of an argument should be presented in a fair way.

bias A disposition of prejudice in favor of a certain idea, person, or perspective.

byline Name of the writer, usually placed between the headline and the story.

chronological order Method of writing a story presenting the details of the story in the order in which they occurred.

column Type of story that is a regular feature, often on a recurring topic, written by the same journalist, generally known as a columnist.

commentary Type of story that is an expression of opinion on recent events by a journalist generally known as a commentator.

credibility The quality of being trustworthy and believable, said of a journalistic source.

editorial Article of opinion or interpretation.

feature story Article designed to entertain as well as to inform.

headline Type, usually 18 point or larger, used to introduce a story.

human interest story Type of story that focuses on individuals and how events or issues affect their life, generally offering a sense of relatability to the reader.

impartiality Principle of journalism that a story should not reflect a journalist's bias and should contain balance.

intention The motive or reason behind something, such as the publication of a news story.

inverted pyramid Method of writing a story using facts in order of importance, beginning with a lead and then gradually adding paragraphs in order of relevance from most interesting to least interesting.

motive The reason behind something, such as the publication of a news story or a source's perspective on an issue.

news story An article or style of expository writing that reports news, generally in a straightforward fashion and without editorial comment.

paraphrase The summary of an individual's words, with attribution, rather than a direct quotation of their exact words.

quotation The use of an individual's exact words indicated by the use of quotation marks and proper attribution.

reliability The quality of being dependable and accurate, said of a journalistic source.

rhetorical device Technique in writing intending to persuade the reader or communicate a message from a certain perspective.

source The origin of the information reported in journalism.

sports reporting Type of story that reports on sporting events or topics related to sports.

style A distinctive use of language in writing or speech; also a news or publishing organization's rules for consistent use of language with regards to spelling, punctuation, typography, and capitalization, usually regimented by a house style guide.

tone A manner of expression in writing or speech.

Media Literacy Questions

1. Identify the various sources cited in the article "When a Soccer Star Falls, It May Be Great Acting" (on page 152). How does Jeffrey Marcus attribute information to each of these sources in his article? How effective are his attributions in helping the reader identify his sources?

2. In "Ronaldo ... for the Defense" (on page 192), Jack Bell directly quotes Cristiano Ronaldo's letter to a judge and prosecutor. What are the strengths of the use of a direct quote as opposed to a paraphrase? What are its weaknesses?

3. Compare the headlines of "Without Ronaldo, No Chance at All" (on page 89) and "Ronaldo's Latest Masterpiece Puts Portugal in Semifinals" (on page 92). Which is a more compelling headline, and why? How could the less compelling headline be changed to better draw the reader's interest?

4. What type of story is "Flash of Red Leaves United Speechless" (on page 59)? Can you identify another article in this collection that is the same type of story?

5. Does Andrew Das demonstrate the journalistic principle of balance/impartiality in his article "Cristiano Ronaldo Banned Five Games for Shoving Referee" (on page 142)? If so, how did he do so? If not, what could he have included to make his article more balanced/impartial?

6. The article "Dear Ronaldo: It Isn't All About You" (on page 148) is an example of an editorial. Identify how Rob Hughes's attitude, tone, and bias help convey his opinion on the topic.

7. Does "With Fame Comes Power for Global Sport" (on page 199) use multiple sources? What are the strengths of using multiple sources in a journalistic piece? What are the weaknesses of relying heavily on one source/few sources?

8. "Ronaldo's Toughest Move" (on page 12) features photographs. What do these photographs add to the article?

9. What type of story is "'Ronaldo's Toughest Move" (on page 12)? Can you identify another article in this collection that is the same type of story?

10. What is the intention of the article "Champions League Final May Settle Ronaldo-Messi Debate" (on page 123)? How effectively does it achieve its intended purpose?

11. Analyze the authors' bias in "Ronaldo May Look Like the Best, but There Is Someone Better" (on page 127) and "Ronaldo Dethrones Messi as World Player of the Year" (on page 139). Do you think one journalist is more biased in their reporting than the other? If so, why do you think so?

12. Often, as a story develops, journalists' attitude toward the subject may change. Compare "Spain Deserves Appreciation, Not Criticism" (on page 55) and "Real Madrid's Emergency Strategy: Leave It to Cristiano Ronaldo (on page 72), both by Rob Hughes. Did new information discovered between the publication of these two articles change his perspective?

13. Identify each of the sources in "How Superstars' Pay Stifles Everyone Else" (on page 171) as a primary source or a secondary source. Evaluate the reliability and credibility of each sources. How does your evaluation of each source change your perspective on this article?

14. In "When a Soccer Star Falls, It May Be Great Acting" (on page 152), Jeffrey Marcus directly quotes various players and referees. What are the strengths of the use of a direct quote as opposed to a paraphrase? What are its weaknesses?

15. What is the intention of the article "In 2017, Many Athletes Found Their Voices" (on page 186)? How effectively does it achieve its intended purpose?

Citations

BOOK CITATION

NEW YORK TIMES EDITORIAL STAFF, THE. *Cristiano Ronaldo.* New York: New York Times Educational Publishing, 2019.

ARTICLE CITATIONS

BELL, JACK. "European Stars to Play for Charity." *The New York Times*, 12 Jan. 2009, http://www.nytimes.com/2009/01/13/sports/soccer/13goal.html.

BELL, JACK. "Ronaldo ... for the Defense." *The New York Times*, 14 Oct. 2013, http://www.nytimes.com/2013/10/15/sports/soccer/ronaldo-for-the-defense.html.

BELL, JACK. "Ronaldo Is Bound for Madrid." *The New York Times*, 11 June 2009, https://goal.blogs.nytimes.com/2009/06/11/ronaldo-is-bound-for-madrid/.

BORDEN, SAM. "At Euro 2016 Final, Portugal Loses Ronaldo but Defeats France." *The New York Times*, 10 July 2016, https://www.nytimes.com/2016/07/11/sports/soccer/euro-2016-portugal-loses-ronaldo-but-defeats-france-in-extra-time.html.

BORDEN, SAM. "Cristiano Ronaldo, Quiet Superstar, Can Win Portugal's Heart With Euros Title." *The New York Times*, 9 July 2016, https://www.nytimes.com/2016/07/10/sports/soccer/cristiano-ronaldo-portugal-euro-2016-final.html.

BORDEN, SAM. "Flash of Red Leaves United Speechless." *The New York Times*, 5 Mar. 2013, http://www.nytimes.com/2013/03/06/sports/soccer/real-madrid-advances-to-champions-league-quarterfinals.html.

BORDEN, SAM. "Portugal Beats Wales at Euro 2016 and Gets Another Shot at Glory." *The New York Times*, 6 July 2016, https://www.nytimes.com/2016/07/07/sports/soccer/portugal-wales-semifinal-cristiano-ronaldo-euro-2016.html.

BORDEN, SAM. "Reprise of '14 Final Has Repeat Result: Real Madrid Wins Championship." *The New York Times*, 28 May 2016, https://www.nytimes.com/2016/05/29/sports/soccer/real-madrid-atletico-madrid-champions-league-final.html.

BORDEN, SAM. "Ronaldo Dethrones Messi as World Player of Year." *The New York Times*, 13 Jan. 2014, https://www.nytimes.com/2014/01/14/sports/soccer/ronaldo-dethrones-messi-as-world-player-of-year.html.

BORDEN, SAM. "Ronaldo's Toughest Move." *The New York Times*, 22 May 2014, https://www.nytimes.com/2014/05/23/sports/soccer/recalling-a-young-cristiano-ronaldo-who-clung-to-his-roots.html.

CHIBBER, KABIR. "Real Madrid Fans' Generational Divide." *The New York Times*, 3 Nov. 2009, https://goal.blogs.nytimes.com/2009/11/03/real-madrid-fans-generational-divide/.

CLAREY, CHRISTOPHER. "In 2017, Many Athletes Found Their Voices." *The New York Times*, 20 Dec. 2017, https://www.nytimes.com/2017/12/20/sports/year-sports-protests.html.

DAS, ANDREW. "Cristiano Ronaldo Banned Five Games for Shoving Referee." *The New York Times*, 14 Aug. 2017, www.nytimes.com/2017/08/14/sports/soccer/cristiano-ronaldo-real-madrid-banned-five-games-referee-shove.html.

DAS, ANDREW. "Messi Named FIFA's Top Player for Fourth Year in a Row." *The New York Times*, 7 Jan. 2013, https://goal.blogs.nytimes.com/2013/01/07/messi-named-fifas-top-player-for-fourth-year-in-a-row/.

DAS, ANDREW. "Portugal vs. Wales Represents More Than Ronaldo Against Bale." *The New York Times*, 5 July 2016, https://www.nytimes.com/2016/07/06/sports/soccer/portugal-vs-wales-represents-more-than-ronaldo-against-bale.html.

HUGHES, ROB. "After World Cup, It's Worlds Apart for Top Players." *The New York Times*, July 18 2010, http://www.nytimes.com/2011/09/14/sports/soccer/14iht-soccer14.html.

HUGHES, ROB. "Dazzling Ronaldo Leaves Arsenal Gasping for Air." *The New York Times*, 15 May 2009, http://www.nytimes.com/2009/05/06/sports/soccer/06soccer.html.

HUGHES, ROB. "Dear Ronaldo: It Isn't All About You." *The New York Times*, 11 Sept. 2012, http://www.nytimes.com/2012/09/12/sports/soccer/12iht-soccer12.html.

HUGHES, ROB. "Genius Has Company in Messi and Ronaldo." *The New York Times*, 16 Nov. 2010, http://www.nytimes.com/2010/11/17/sports/soccer/17iht-SOCCER.html.

HUGHES, ROB. "In European Soccer, World Cup Is One of Many Priorities." *The New York Times*, 22 Oct. 2013, http://www.nytimes.com/2013/10/23/sports/soccer/in-european-soccer-focus-is-on-champions-league.html.

HUGHES, ROB. "In Europe, Young, Gifted and Limping." *The New York Times*, 20 Sept. 2011, http://www.nytimes.com/2011/09/21/sports/soccer/21iht-soccer21.html.

HUGHES, ROB. "Madrid and Ronaldo Give Happiness a Chance." *The New York Times*, 19 Sept. 2012, http://www.nytimes.com/2012/09/20/sports/soccer/20iht-soccer20.html.

HUGHES, ROB. "Messi and Ronaldo: 2 Stars in Their Own Universe." *The New York Times*, 8 Oct. 2012, http://www.nytimes.com/2012/10/09/sports/soccer/09iht-soccer09.html.

HUGHES, ROB. "Real Madrid's Emergency Strategy: Leave It to Cristiano Ronaldo." *The New York Times*, 13 Apr. 2016, https://www.nytimes.com/2016/04/14/sports/soccer/real-madrid-cristiano-ronaldo-wolfsburg.html.

HUGHES, ROB. "Real Madrid Wins Ugly in an Un-Classic Barcelona Clásico." *The New York Times*, 3 Apr. 2016, https://www.nytimes.com/2016/04/04/sports/soccer/real-madrid-wins-ugly-in-un-classic-barcelona-clasico.html.

HUGHES, ROB. "Ronaldo and Messi Reign in Spain." *The New York Times*, 24 Oct. 2011, http://www.nytimes.com/2011/10/24/sports/soccer/24iht-soccer24.html.

HUGHES, ROB. "Ronaldo Leaves His Old Team in Awe." *The New York Times*, 14 Feb. 2013, http://www.nytimes.com/2013/02/15/sports/soccer/15iht-soccer15.html.

HUGHES, ROB. "Ronaldo May Look Like the Best, but There Is Someone Better." *The New York Times*, 13 Sept. 2011, http://www.nytimes.com/2011/09/14/sports/soccer/14iht-soccer14.html.

HUGHES, ROB. "Ronaldo's Latest Masterpiece Puts Portugal in Semifinals." *The New York Times*, 21 June 2012, http://www.nytimes.com/2012/06/22/sports/soccer/euro-2012-ronaldo-leads-portugal-past-czech-republic.html.

HUGHES, ROB. "Ronaldo Struts Across Big Stage." *The New York Times*, 5 May 2009, http://www.nytimes.com/2009/05/06/sports/soccer/06iht-SOCCER.html.

HUGHES, ROB. "Ronaldo to Join Real Madrid for Record Price." *The New York Times*, 11 June 2009, http://www.nytimes.com/2009/06/12/sports/soccer/12iht-RONALDO.html.

HUGHES, ROB. "Spain Deserves Appreciation, Not Criticism." *The New York Times*, 26 June, 2012, http://www.nytimes.com/2012/06/27/sports/soccer/27iht-soccer27.html.

HUGHES, ROB. "Still Waiting to See Cristiano Ronaldo's Brilliance." *The New*

York Times, 5 July 2016, https://www.nytimes.com/2016/07/06/sports/soccer/cristiano-ronaldo-euros-waiting-for-his-brilliance.html.

HUGHES, ROB. "3 Modern Soccer Gods and One Bad Apple." *The New York Times*, 24 Oct. 2010, http://www.nytimes.com/2010/10/25/sports/soccer/25iht-SOCCER.html.

HUGHES, ROB. "A Top Performance Before the Clásico." *The New York Times*, 23 Oct. 2014, https://www.nytimes.com/2014/10/24/sports/soccer/a-top-performance-before-the-clsico.html.

HUGHES, ROB. "A Victory for Haves (Real) vs. Have-Nots (Roma)." *The New York Times*, 28 Feb. 2016, https://www.nytimes.com/2016/02/19/sports/soccer/a-victory-for-haves-real-vs-have-nots-roma.html.

HUGHES, ROB. "With Fame Comes Power for Global Sports Stars." *The New York Times*, 10 July 2009, http://www.nytimes.com/2009/07/11/sports/soccer/11iht-hughes.html.

HUGHES, ROB. "Without Ronaldo, No Chance at All." *The New York Times*, 28 June 2012, http://www.nytimes.com/2012/06/29/sports/soccer/29iht-hughes29.html.

KEH, ANDREW. "Ronaldo, Under Fire, Strikes Quickly Before Slipping Away." *The New York Times*, 21 June 2017, https://www.nytimes.com/2017/06/21/sports/soccer/cristiano-ronaldo-spain-tax-fraud.html.

LONGMAN, JERÉ. "After Slump, Ronaldo's Goals Come in Bunches." *The New York Times*, 17 June 2012, http://www.nytimes.com/2012/06/18/sports/soccer/euro-2012-after-slow-start-ronaldo-advances-portugal-with-2-goals.html.

LONGMAN, JERÉ. "Champions League Final May Settle Ronaldo-Messi Debate." *The New York Times*, 26 May 2009, http://www.nytimes.com/2009/05/27/sports/soccer/27soccer.html.

LONGMAN, JERÉ. "Despite a Hex, Ronaldo Works Magic." *The New York Times*, 22 June 2014, https://www.nytimes.com/2014/06/23/sports/worldcup/world-cup-2014-cristiano-ronaldo-defies-a-witch-doctor.html.

MARCUS, JEFFREY. " 'Ronaldo Is the Most Annoying.' " *The New York Times*, 10 Dec. 2010, https://goal.blogs.nytimes.com/2010/12/10/ronaldo-is-the-most-annoying/.

MARCUS, JEFFREY. "Ronaldo on Track to Eclipse Beckham's Riches." *The New York Times*, 22 Apr. 2010, https://goal.blogs.nytimes.com/2010/04/22/ronaldo-on-track-to-eclipse-beckhams-riches/.

MARCUS, JEFFREY. "A Victory for Portugal, but a Disappointment for Ronaldo."

The New York Times, 14 June 2012, https://goal.blogs.nytimes.com/2012/06/14/a-victory-for-portugal-but-a-disappointment-for-ronaldo/.

MARCUS, JEFFREY. "When A Soccer Star Falls, It May Be Great Acting." *The New York Times,* 20 June 2010, http://www.nytimes.com/2010/06/21/sports/soccer/21diving.html?pagewanted=1.

PORTER, EDUARDO. "How Superstars' Pay Stifles Everyone Else." *The New York Times,* 25 Dec. 2010, http://www.nytimes.com/2010/12/26/business/26excerpt.html.

SMITH, RORY. "At Real Madrid, a Reign Fueled by Wins, and Dependent on More." *The New York Times,* 14 Feb. 2018, https://www.nytimes.com/2018/02/14/sports/soccer/real-madrid-florentinoperez.html?action=click&contentCollection=Sports&module=RelatedCoverage&region=EndOfArticle&pgtype=article.

SMITH, RORY. "In Loss to Real Madrid, P.S.G. Fails on the Big Stage It Covets." *The New York Times,* 14 Feb. 2018, https://www.nytimes.com/2018/02/14/sports/in-loss-to-real-madrid-psg-fails-on-the-big-stage-it-covets.html.

SMITH, RORY. " ' Made in Sporting': Lisbon Club's Youth Academy Sets It Apart." *The New York Times,* 21 Nov. 2016, https://www.nytimes.com/2016/11/21/sports/soccer/soccer-sporting-lisbon-youth-academy.html.

SMITH, RORY. "Real Madrid, Hard to Define, Firms Its Stamp on Champions League." *The New York Times,* 3 June 2017, https://www.nytimes.com/2017/06/03/sports/soccer/champions-league-real-madrid-juventus.html.

VECSEY, GEORGE. "The Rain and the Minutes Pelt Down." *The New York Times,* 22 May 2008, http://www.nytimes.com/2008/05/22/sports/soccer/22vecsey.html.

WIDDICOMBE, BEN. "Poparazzi | The Manly Business of Gossip." *The New York Times,* 13 July 2010, https://tmagazine.blogs.nytimes.com/2010/07/13/poparazzi-the-manly-business-of-gossip/.

WILSON, ERIC. "Nice Goal! How'd You Like to Be a Model?" *The New York Times,* 7 July 2010, http://www.nytimes.com/2010/07/08/fashion/08ROW.html.

Index